Star-Struck Teenage ALIEN

by

Jane Greenhill

Star-Struck Teenage ALIEN

Cover Art by *Jennifer Greeff*

The Wild Rose Press, Inc.
PO Box 708
Adams Basin, NY 14410-0708
Visit us at www.thewildrosepress.com

Publishing History
First Edition, 2021
Trade Paperback ISBN 978-1-5092-3666-4
Digital ISBN 978-1-5092-3667-1

Published in the United States of America

How lucky can you get when the mawl you like is crazy for you and looks good in any life form, be it insect or humanoid? When I first met Josh, we were in an ice cream store on Earth, and I ate the wicked ice cream way too fast and got a brain freeze. Not a good way to impress. But when his brown curly hair and the two little indents on either side of his mouth appeared as he came to my rescue, I was a goner. Yep, I loved his cute accent, loved his cute tush, and just loved, loved, loved the mawl.

"I love you, Josh."

"Sorry, did you say something?" Josh asked, the two dents appearing even in Zorcan form.

Crap! Double crap! Triple crap! And whatever crap could come after that. How could I be so stupid, such an idiot as to say that out loud? I didn't need my *mist book* to know that I'd screwed up big time. Never—no matter what solar system you're in—you shouldn't be the first to tell anyone—especially a mawl as cute as Josh—that you love them. He said nothing, so I picked at the red carpet, pulling out threads from a T until it looked like an I.

"Really? You're not just saying that?" Josh's voice came out soft and really sweet.

So, he had heard me.

Dedication

To Geoff: my world, my universe, my all.

Chapter 1

Major hangover.

Major freakin' hangover.

Major throbbing, major pain in the thorax, or as you Earthlings refer to it, a neck stomach area. You know the kind of brain meltdown you encounter when you've partied too much, mixed too many carbonated beverages—not in a good way—and then kept them all down?

My mandibles and legs ached. Muscles I didn't even know could throb were sore. My three eyes felt so heavy I could hardly keep them open. My head rested on something hard. I groggily turned over, weak and stunned, and was somewhat relieved to find it was my *hanaglug*, my interplanetary traveling suitcase which disappears when I don't require it, given to me by Zen, my handler.

For a highly evolved praying mantis, I was in rough shape.

Barely alive.

Just by the skin of my teeth.

My stomach contents swirled around like I was on an upside-down rollercoaster, the cars spinning out of control, the handbrake not slowing the speed at all.

Let's just say I felt like crap, and you know who I had to thank for it.

I'm sure I don't have to tell you if you have one or

two (or six hundred ninety-eight, like I do) and a heck of a lot of the number are mawls, or as you Earthlings call them, boys.

Have you guessed yet?

My sibling.

Yes indeed, my brother Ralb was the reason for my major discontent.

Revenge would be slow, painful, and merciless. Maybe bamboo shoots under his dirty, yucky fingernails or…

I'm not violent, far from it. It's not like I wanted to kill him or anything, just make his life a living heck.

Payback!

And I could. And I would.

Beginning now.

My brother and I have a major love-hate, basically can't-to-be-in-the-same-room-as-each-other
relationship. But in my defense, how would you feel if you were the brains in the family, yet you were forced to stay on your lame home planet because he was a mawl and, therefore, the one sent to Earth? No doubt you'd be ticked too. Then you were told and, not too nicely I might add, to go and bring him home because he'd fallen for an Earthling and didn't want to leave. So, long story short, being the dutiful—ahem—loving sister I am, I put my own life on hold and space-traveled to your planet to bring him home, like he was a lost puppy. I'd like to crate him to keep him out of trouble…

Then, and, through no fault of my own, I fell in love.

With Josh.

But even then, I placed the well-being of my planet

ahead of my own selflessness (unlike others I might mention), and, after I said a sad farewell to my loved one, Ralb and I climbed to the top of the silo and waited for the lightning bolt to energize us home.

Well, that didn't happen. Not by a long sling shot.

My brother Ralb is the worst navigator of any mawl I've ever encountered. It's an undisputed truth across this galaxy and three constellations that he could get lost on a sidewalk on a sunny day. Though from what I understand from listening to my *wad*, which picks up all your Earth television shows, mawls on your planet don't like to ask for directions either. Maybe it's universal!! So why did the elders of my planet think he could get us home in one piece? He must have brainwashed them or given them a Zorcan mind melting.

He claimed he aimed for our home planet, but instead we took a wrong turn at the Black Hole. Not once, but twice. The first time we ended up in France. Not that I'm really complaining. Well, not much. I met Jason Montana but blew him off to visit with Josh, my Earth mawlfriend, who flew to France on a holiday with his Parental Being. I know, like, talk about major coincidence. Long story even shorter, Josh and I kissed, and he turned into a praying mantis. Not because of my kiss, mind you. It's not like I'm some kind of a freak or a witch who turns her mawlfriends into insects, even if that would be kind of cool. Especially if it was someone you really didn't like.

I guess it would be the ultimate French kiss.

No, like siblings all across the universe, Ralb ruined the moment. Josh and I were finally alone, but, stupid me, I turned my back on my bro and he tossed freezing salt water on us. Salt causes me to change from humanoid to insect or vice versa. So next thing I know, I'm lying on a *tres* uncomfortable red carpet, here.

Wherever the heck here might be.

Chapter 2

From what I can see, I'm a heck of a long way from home. This was definitely not Zorca-twenty-three, my home planet, three stars from the Space Port. For one thing, as far as my three-eye mantis form can see, glamor and glitz abounded. My planet was made up of rocks, rocks, and you guessed it more rocks, not to mention highly evolved praying mantis. Like *moi*.

I scanned humanoid mawls who were in tuxes, the regulation black-and-white outfit grooms wear on Earth wedding days, making them eye candy but not enough to distract from the main attraction. The femawls slinking along the carpet were decked out in heavily beaded gowns, all borrowed, of course, from the designers who wanted to be in this week's tabloid magazine.

From my vantage point on the smelly red carpet, I had a three-eye view as broadcasters from every major network elbowed each other out of the way.

Heavy, clunky, red velvet drapes hung alongside huge fans weaving unsteadily on white stands. The whirling produced a slight breeze but didn't stir the fabric one iota. Black wrought iron guardrails tipped with gold twined in the shape of the TZZ logo kept the public away from the glittery movie and television stars. What can I say? I'm slightly addicted to entertainment shows and magazines.

Massive concrete planters, with the TZZ logo chiseled into them, adorned the carpet, sitting like soldiers every five meters. Filled to capacity and overflowing with dahlias, cannas, hibiscus, and—could it be? A bird's foot trefoil flower, my femawl Parental Being's favorite flower.

I snugged my butt against the planter, the bird's foot trefoil trailed over my body, covering me, protecting me. Aww, the fragrance reminded me of home.

****

From my vantage point, I tried to figure out who the camera people were trying to capture with their cameras and microphones. Was it the latest teen idol, whose hair never moved even in a wind tunnel? (Yes, it had been tested.)

Rumbles turned to whispers as I overheard and felt the excitement as the most talked about outfit of the night turned the corner.

The commentators were babbling loudly enough to make eavesdropping easy, especially with my *wad*. According to them, Wong Chow Lu was the IT designer, and his dress (and I'm using major antenna quotes here) was to "die for," though personally I wouldn't die or even faint for it.

One-and-a-half meters of sparkly black lace and taffeta adorned with feathers had been tweaked and tucked to barely cover the wearer's bits, crisscrossing across the front and back like a roll of gaudy, glittery tape gone wild.

The commentators then gushed about the feathers, which had been flown in from a remote monastery in the Himalayas. Colors unseen by anyone but the priests had been hand sewn to the corset in rainbow patterns replicating the Rockhopper penguin, an endangered species that the wearer had adopted as her own personal cause. Emeralds and rubies competed as the decorations for the penguin eyes. A remote-control device, cleverly hidden inside the purse, clutched by the undisputed Center of Attention, caused the feathers to puff like a lovesick penguin. Long yellow feathers tied to her hair whispered in the slight breeze.

I mean, who in their right mind would wear something like that in public? I knew who. I didn't need anyone to tell me.

And there she was, strutting down the runway like she was a beauty pageant winner. Every eye focused on her purple hair (which has been compared to lilacs, but to me looked more like prunes) and her puffing penguin feathers. And her penguin "tail", which must have spanned ten meters, almost took out a camerawoman's eye when she swished and preened for photographs.

Yes, America's annoying teen-pop-star-slash-television-star and, if my vibes are on the correct wavelength—which they always are—we'll also be adding reality star.

I'm sure you've heard of her, seen her, and smelled her new line of fragrances. Suzzy Newsworthy, or Sn to her league of followers.

Flashbulbs singed my eyes like rabid fireflies, their aftereffect causing black dots to dance across all three of my eyes. I blinked repeatedly, but when my eyes cleared, I was hit with another barrage of lightning. It was like I was in the middle of a summer heat storm, blasting through my Zorca-twenty-three planet.

But no, blame it on the fifteen disco balls hung

from a canopy of white silk, their colors creating sparks radiating a neon rainbow, accenting (not clashing with) the colors of Suzzy Newsworthy's breathtakingly newsworthy attire.

I, for one, knew everything there was to know about the TZZ's, presented in Las Vegas, Nevada, as I watched them every year via my *wad* from the comfort of my bedroom rock on Zorca-twenty-three, dressed in my jammiejo's.

Which reminded me. If I was here, Ralb must be too. And as much as I wasn't the number one fan (or two or three) of my bro, I could certainly use some company. Stars, at this point, I would even feel grateful I had a brother. Man, do desperate times ever call for desperate measures.

A cough distracted me. I peeked through the foliage to see who was sharing my oxogyen.

As my tired eyes focused, my heart leaped through my thorax. Not my bothersome bro. Even better. Yes, it was my mawlfriend.

Josh!

And he was in Zorca-twenty-three form rather than the humanoid one I'd originally fallen in love with.

Chapter 3

"Josh, oh thank stars, you're here and okay!" I shimmied over to where he sat beside the planter, dragging my *hanaglug*. I squeezed him like I'd seen humanoids do with their toothpaste. The pleasant aroma of body wash twittered my antennas, reminding me of my first trip to Earth. Josh had been sweet and kind, and he hadn't treated me like an alien even when he found out I was. Unlike other teenage mawls—okay, the only one I could compare him to was my brother Ralb, and he probably wasn't a good example—Josh was…nice. And okay, majorly cute.

"Hey, Oas, wasn't that quite the ride?" Josh reached over to give me a mini-massage, rubbing my antennas in a way that tingled my goose bumps.

And let me tell you, when a mawl gives you goose bumps on your scales—when your mawlfriends on your home planet never caused them—he's definitely a keeper.

"I knew you were unique when I met you, but you've shown me a whole new world. Totally awesome." Josh puffed out his taunt mantis abdomen, long and firm, an abdomen that looked like he went to the gym regularly and not just to sit on the equipment.

"Josh, I'm sorry you had to go through that. My brother Ralb isn't the most—"

"Don't apologize, Oas."

He twined his antenna around mine, and it was beyond heaven. Beyond extraterrestrial. Even Gorget, my ex-mawlfriend from Zorca-twenty-three, who thought he was the hottest mawl in the solar system, couldn't hold a burning stick to the feelings Josh ignited.

"But how did you end up here?" I shook my head, trying to figure out the *linguistics*. Salt doesn't affect humans other than to cause water retention.

"Maybe it was that pill you gave me in France, the one where I could see you in your true form?" Josh rubbed the inside of my mandible, sending a quiver up my backbone and excessive throbbing to all three of my eyes.

Josh squeezed me tightly. I sucked in my stomach and fluttered all my eyelashes. My middle eye twitched in what I hoped was an attractive and not totally gross way. He moved closer and rubbed his wings against mine, causing major friction and a shock creating a spark. I guess I must not have created a gross eyelashes flutter, then.

He was the cutest praying mantis I'd ever laid eyes on, and if you knew how densely populated my planet is, you'd be impressed. I know I sure was.

How lucky can you get when the mawl you like is crazy for you and looks good in any life form, be it insect or humanoid? When I first met Josh, we were in an ice cream store on Earth, and I ate the wicked ice cream way too fast and got a brain freeze. Not a good way to impress. But when his brown curly hair and the two little indents on either side of his mouth appeared as he came to my rescue, I was a goner. Yep, I loved his cute accent, loved his cute tush, and just loved, loved,

loved the mawl.

"I love you, Josh."

"Sorry, did you say something?" Josh asked, the two dents appearing even in Zorcan form.

Crap! Double crap! Triple crap! And whatever crap could come after that. How could I be so stupid, such an idiot as to say that out loud? I didn't need my *mist book* to know that I'd screwed up big time. Never—no matter what solar system you're in—you shouldn't be the first to tell anyone—especially a mawl as cute as Josh—that you love them. He said nothing, so I picked at the red carpet, pulling out threads from a *T* until it looked like an *I*.

"Really? You're not just saying that?" Josh's voice came out soft and really sweet.

So, he had heard me.

"Hey, didn't I dump Jason Montana for you?" I grinned. "Not a lot of girls would pass up coffee with him. But I did. For you." *Oh stars!* I feel like a royal fool. What do I do? I don't want to trick him into saying it, do I? Now I'm turning into Suzz, Ralb's Earth g-friend, willing to do any kind of trick to snag a mawl.

"True," Josh said. "Heck, I *would* pass up time with me to meet him, so I'm very impressed."

"Yeah, well, I'm impressed with you too."

"You are?" His face turned the purple color of a Zorcan harvest moon.

"Are you fishing for compliments, or what?" I winked my left eye.

"Naw." The red tinge spread across all ten millimeters of his body. He shuffled his mandibles and looked toward the crowd. "We're definitely not still in France. So, where are we?"

All around us gold sequins and stilettos abounded. Heavily beaded brocade dresses, which probably tipped the scales at more than my earthly weight, floated by on perfect bodies, each figure with more suction and lift than the previous.

"My brother miscalculated. Again. We're at—"

Josh interrupted, "Wow, look at all the famous people here. Are those the actors from the movie *Stars Above*?"

"Are you searching for Suzzy Newsworthy?" I spit out the name like it was poison on my forked tongue. "She's up for several awards." A totally unnecessary comment. Everyone in both your solar system and mine knew she was the most popular star on the red carpet.

"Why would I be looking for her? The hottest chick—umm, bug—in the universe is right here beside me." He flicked my chin with his antenna and then sweetly slipped his antenna around mine.

Aww. He hadn't said the three words I wanted to hear, but if he was on my planet, his actions would make us almost married. But I didn't have time to enjoy the pleasing sensations sizzling like a steak on a grill in my abdomen.

A screech from the microphone interrupted our romantic rendezvous.

John Stonegate, the host from the top-rated reality show *Deal Breaker*, waved the mic for attention and then spoke with great fanfare. "And now the moment you've all been waiting for. The reigning queen of pop, Suzzy Newsworthy, is heeeeeere in person!"

The contents of my stomach spiraled out of control. Just the mere mention of her name triggered the urge to upchuck. I covered my antennas; the screaming from the female fans was enough to pierce my supersensitive sensors.

"...whose television show *Suzzy Newsworthy Stars Above* was a huge hit with the pre-teens. At the age of sixteen, she'd already signed three record deals with six albums going platinum and had a TV show that took ten Youth Winner Awards. She has homes on each continent, all decorated identically so she feels at home no matter what country she is visiting. But I don't need to tell you all that. She's a star amongst stars."

She was a phony; her accent was a put on, as was the sweetness for the cameras.

And she was my brother Ralb's girlfriend.

Suzz had obviously been in the *Conceited* line when they handed out personality traits. She was friends with my BFF Nicola, and Suzz would step on anything and anyone who got in her way. Her public sweetness and put-on accent were as fake as the wig perched on her head.

Long story even shorter, I'd met her in Bedrocktown when I'd come to rescue my brother from her clutches and discovered the town was being poisoned by an *E. coli* outbreak. My bad. I thought it was caused by her father's farm, but alas they were innocent. But with the news exposure to Bedrocktown, she was discovered. And did she ever thank me? No. Never one to miss an opportunity, but faster than you can say *E. coli* she reinvented herself signing any contract passing under her pen. Talk about an overnight sensation. You might wonder how I know this when I was time-traveling, let's just say my *wad* is worth more than its weight. I still can't figure out the time zone time-traveling situation. My planet counts eons and you

Earthlings count years which is waaaaayyy too much math for this praying mantis. AND I was only supposed to be here for a certain period of time, but between eons and years, something got messed up big time and I'm still here, you're welcome.

"Let's give a big Las Vegas welcome to the reigning teen star of H-wood, our very own Suzzy Newsworthy, accompanied by her manager Beau Richardson. Thank you for taking the time to talk to us and to your adoring public, Suzzy," John Stonegate groveled. Obviously, the man was smart enough to know his nighttime ratings would quadruple just from having the tanning-bed-addict-slash-always-perfect-hair-and-skin femawl share the stage with him.

Beau Richardson! I couldn't help myself. I elongated myself up for a glance. Highlighted hair, parted on the side, covered his forehead. Eyes the color of a Caribbean sky, a nose with a history of being broken, a chin dimple I could fit my baby finger in (not that I would try if given the opportunity or anything), and lips that smirked in every picture I'd ever seen. A leer that left everyone thinking he knew something they didn't, that he'd gotten away with something your mother would never want to know. Not that I was interested or anything. I had my Josh. But I'm just saying, for a humanoid, he was a fine specimen.

If a tad too cocky for my tastes.

"Oh John, you just dill my pickle," Suzzy Newsworthy drawled, making the last three words fifteen syllables. "It should be li'l old me thanking you for talking to *moi*." She pushed a jewel on her purse that puffed and depuffed her penguin feathers flirtatiously. She shifted the black, ankle-length material to reveal bright orange cowboy boots. She cracked and smacked a wad of gum, blowing a large bubble before collapsing it back inside her cheeks. "I really don't have much to chat your little ear off about."

Her bogus accent was as thick as the bologna she was spreading around so liberally.

"Oh, Suzzy, I'm sure our viewers would disagree, don't you all agree?" He gestured for a roaring, clapping response. He clasped her arm to pull her closer to the masking-tape X on the carpet. "Now, what has our little filly been up to these days? You've cut your latest album—which climbed to number one with the hit, 'Gotta Hate those Aliens,' completed a tour of the Asian countries, and if the rumors are true, got a tattoo of a penguin on your lower back."

Suzzy giggled and preened for the camera. "And, John, don't forget my brand of gum. It's called 'Sn's Got Your Tongue', and it's available in five tantalizing flavors. Just this past week we released sugar beet, black currant, almond chocolate, caramel pecan, and popcorn." She paused. "And my gum has a secret ingredient in it, so you don't have to brush your teeth. It's grittier than normal gum. Okay, I'll spill the beanso. It contains a dash of sea salt. My fans love, love, love, love, love, *love* it."

"Wow, Suzzy. A lot of superstars have their own brand of perfumes, and your brand has outsold the top five combined. What made you decide to get into bubblegum?"

"Well, John," she said with a giggle. "As you know, I fly an awful lot, and my little old ears would sometimes not pop. Kinda funny when you think of it, here I am a pop star and my ears don't." She squealed like a pig at the trough. "So I thought why the hayfield not create great gum?"

"Are you going to be home in one of your identical homes to rest for a while after your whirlwind tour?" he asked.

Suzzy Newsworthy popped another bubble, the gum crackling like an evil witch's laugh. "Actually, John," she said, clutching his arm, "I've decided to do some more traveling."

"Really?" The rapt attention he was paying her would have been worth the price of admission, if I'd paid to get in here. "I thought you'd already visited all seven continents?"

"Well, you're plum-tooting right." Suzzy yanked at his tie. "But I haven't been above them," she added coyly. "My manager thinks it's about time I"—giggle— "expand my horizons even further."

"You have me totally bamboozled here." John straightened his tie and tucked it back inside his black silk jacket. "You must have been above it in your Lear." He paused. "Are you playing with me, Suzzy Newsworthy?"

"You're as dang foolish as a one-armed hanger at a fashion show. No, silly goosekins, I'm going cruising by Antarctica, waving a hello to the Rockhopper penguins." She paused. "I hope one of them doesn't hit us flying."

"Umm, Suzzy, penguins don't fly." John whispered.

Ignoring him she continued. "My new song 'Rock'n Hopp'n Penguins' is already number one right along with the flipping flapping scooting dance craze." She flapped her arms and bent down to cradle her knees. "I'm heading into space, outer space."

"What?" He feigned surprise, a feat that should have earned him his own acting award.

You had to have lived in a different solar system not to have heard the news, and I do. You need to get yourself a *wad*. Suzzy Newsworthy's space flight was the subject of every talk show on the planet, front page on every weekly tabloid, and had even made the six o'clock news in H-wood, a slot usually reserved for blood and guts. Heck, even I knew about it, and I'd been in France.

Suzzy Newsworthy leaned closer and whispered in John's ear but made sure she was turned so her words carried into the microphone. "I'm in top-secret talks right now, but I can let you in on a tiny little surprise, something that hasn't been released yet to the general public."

I covered my mouth with my grasping front legs to suppress my laughter. Who was she kidding? Did the old Suzz, now Suzzy Newsworthy, really think she could pull the cotton over our eyes?

She paused dramatically. "We're killing two birds with one rock. First of all"—she counted on her fingers— "you're the only one to hear this outside my circle. I'm starring in a reality show called *Suzzy's Take on Space*."

"And two—"

I'm sure I'm not the only one who was surprised she could count that high, but then again, she was using her fingers.

"I'm set to star in a movie called *Suzzy Newsworthy Conquers the Stars*, so my manager thought it would be great exposure for me"—she stopped to giggle and, without taking a breath, continued— "to travel in space. Later tonight after the after-parties, I'll be launching into space with two other civilians, and we're going to hook up with the Space Port."

Wha-a-a-t? Did I hear her say Space Port? The Space Port was just a short hop, skip, and a few wing beats from my home planet of Zorca-twenty-three. Woohoo, if I played my cards right, we could hitch a ride and be back home before the first moon came up. It might finally become a benefit to me. I have to say I'm not too impressed with it so far, the light shines right into my bedroom and is sooo annoying.

Zorca-twenty-three. Rocks and a desert climate might not sound like heaven to you, but to me it was. My Parental Beings were there, and I wanted to show off my planet to Josh.

"Who are the lucky people?" John Stonegate's question forced me to quit my happy dance and concentrate on what Suzzy was saying.

How much money would I have to fork over to secure a seat on her high-priced tour bus—er, rocketship? Maybe I could rely on our history, remind her of the good times we had. Umm, there was the time she made fun of my hair, or the time she bullied me about my clothes. Or maybe the time when she called me an ugly bug and said it would never work out with Ralb because her family would never approve of him once they discovered I was his sister. On third thought, maybe I could sneak aboard as an intergalactic hitchhiker.

"Beau Richardson and the winner of our Suzzy Newsworthy's *So You Wanna Be Me* contest are the lucky ones to share space seats with me, but only to a certain altitude. So, they won't need no training, we'll just be floating around like bubbles in a glass of champagne."

"Wish I was going." His face turned a shade of green I've always associated with vomit as she raced on, seemingly oblivious to his discontent.

"When I get the word from Mission Central, they'll advise me to leave the main capsule and crawl into the minipod. Then I'll be catapulted off into a higher atmosphere and into orbit heading straight for the Space Port."

Shock spread across his face. "Umm, isn't there some training involved? They can't take any person off the street, especially one as beautiful and famous as you, and throw them into SpaceMoonOne and let them head up to visit the man in the moon."

"You just curdle my grits, you do." She played with the clasp on her beaded clutch purse. "Of course, I've had extensive training, which, to summarize a bit, involves learning to survive when you're floating around in zippo gravity." She laughed. "As far as my co-travelers are concerned, they won't be up any higher than an airplane, roughly thirty thousand feet." Her feathers swayed with her button pushing. "Wong kindly created a custom-made spacesuit for me, and a T-shirt clothing line with cool space sayings will be available through my website." Looking directly into the camera, she pointed. "View my daily podcast and see my new line firsthand, then head over to my security-encoded website where you can purchase a copy of my daily collectable saying T-shirt with any major credit card."

Wow, the girl from Bedrocktown had turned into a

marketing guru.

"It's unbelievable they're letting you go up." He paused, the incredulity in his voice echoing my thoughts. "The insurance must be insane. Anyone else going along?"

"Duh, like I told you who was coming." She sighed and rolled her eyes heavenward. "Doesn't that just fry your green tomatoes?" She buffed her fingernails. "Can you imagine what the contest winner will be experiencing?"

"Traveling to space would be pretty awesome," Beau Richardson, her manager agreed.

"Well, yeah, there's that too, but I meant spending time with me."

John Stonegate pinched his lips as if trapping a fruit fly. "That definitely would be an added perk." He rearranged his facial expression and continued. "So, with the reality show, the T-shirt line, and the movie, I guess that's about all you've got on your very full platter." The camerawoman rolled her empty hand at John. Last year's Asocar winner was heading toward the podium.

Obviously in no hurry to move along, the old Suzz I remembered so well prattled on, "Also, I get to smash a bottle of champagne against the side of a new TZZ satellite during my own mini-space walk."

"Are you sure?" John Stonegate asked. "With zero gravity and all? Unbelievable."

"You bet your grandmother's dentures I am." Suzzy Newsworthy cracked her gum. "Ikey Newton from Control Central told me I was going to pop a cork when I got up there. What else could he mean?"

Suppressing a smile, the interviewer

absentmindedly combed his fingers through his gel-styled hair. "I think he meant…oh, never mind. To wrap up, Suzzy, just think in a few short hours you'll be spinning through space encased in a metal tube on your way to the Space Port. Are you nervous?"

"I asked the guy training me if there was a way that they could put a stop to the spinning." She cracked her gum.

"I guess he said no." John gave the waiting celebrity an apologetic glance.

"*Au contraire, mon ami.*" She blew a bubble. "He assured me he personally would make sure there was absolutely, positively no turning, rotating, or twirling."

"And did this font of assurance give you his name?"

"Yes, he did. Don't you listen? I said his name was Ikey Newton, and I'm to call him if I need any help when I'm on board."

John Stonegate hid a smile behind one hand. "Yes, I'm sure you should."

Suzzy flicked a red punch-colored curl off her shoulder and paused. "I can't wait to see Earth from space. Ikey said I'd be able to see the Great Wall of China."

"Yes, it's the only one of the seven world wonders you can see from above the Earth." John moved the mike away, trying to wrap up the interview.

But she sidled closer. "Kinda tooting hilarious when you think of it, because I played Wonder Cat in my latest movie, and I'm about to view the Seventh Wonder. Kind of like a Wonder seeing a Wonder."

"Wow, that's quite the experience for one so young." John Stonegate put his arm across her shoulders and attempted to move her off the mark and off camera.

She shrugged him off. "John, I live to play and play to live. Life is what you make it, and I intend to make everyday count when I'm on this earth." She threw up her arms and lost her balance, falling sideways off the stage.

John grabbed for her and ended up with a huge handful of feathers. Audience and celebrities alike fell silent as John sheepishly placed part of the dress back on the stage.

Fighting to regain her composure, Suzzy loomed over me. With the fleet-of-feet known to my species, I ducked and scooted under the rim of a planter and the shelter of its overhanging greenery. As Suzzy fell, her left boob popped out of her corset, and the wad of tissues she'd used to pump up her bra size fell out.

Apparently oblivious to the drama around us, Josh bit his lip and said, "There's something I'd like to say to you." He took a deep breath. "April, I've never said this to anyone before, except my mom, and my dad before he died."

"What?" I asked. I admit, looking back on our conversation, I was distracted.

Watching Suzzy Newsworthy-slash-Suzz make a royal fool of herself was fun. It's not every day you get to see someone who has made your Earth life a living heck being the butt of the joke. I was enjoying every minute, every second, of it. It took me a minute to realize he'd called me by my Earth name of APRIL which stands for Alien Person Representing Intelligent Life and not my Zorca-twenty-three name of Oas. That should have told me how serious he was about what he was about to say.

Hastily, Suzzy Newsworthy stuffed everything back into its proper space and struggled to stand, and stand she did, hands behind her back to cover her exposed rump roast.

"April, I'll just say it. I—"

Although I'd stayed protected under the overhang of the drooping petals, Josh hadn't been so fortunate.

Suzzy staggered, losing her balance. She grabbed at the planter but caught only foliage. The contents slipped through her fingers, giving her zero leverage. Instead, she staggered backward, her cowboy boots headed straight for Josh.

Suzzy Newsworthy stepped on him and squished him like a bug.

Chapter 4

Suzzy Newsworthy killed my mawlfriend.

Suzzy Newsworthy née Suzz stamped out Josh.

She exterminated him and then picked up a penguin feather and wiped his corpse from the bottom of her boot like he was roadkill, or rather, red-carpet kill.

My heart felt on fire, ripped out and stomped on by heavy work boots before being thrust back inside my body raging at five hundred degrees Fahrenheit.

She scraped him off her hot orange boots on the podium and then had the nerve to grin up at the television camera and climb back up the step.

"Well, tie me to an anthill and fill my ears with honey, honey. I don't know if I'll be able to turn in these here boots at the end of the night," she admitted to John Stonegate. "However, if Wong won't accept the return of the boots, I'll purchase them myself and sell them on my website, the proceeds going to Suzzy Newsworthy's Home for the Aged. I really think it's important to look after old people because, well, they're old and can't really look after themselves."

Last year's Asocar winner strode past the stage, his posture indicating he was offended, even I as an alien could tell when someone was mighty ticked off.

John obviously needed Suzz to fill up the air space. He grimaced down at Josh, or rather what had been

Josh. "Can you confirm the rumors you were paid more than sixteen million dollars for your latest movie?"

"Well, my agent thought it was pretty darn tooting cool I got one cool mil for every year of my life."

Snap! I couldn't believe she was so shallow, discussing her bank account when she'd just murdered my mawlfriend.

In cold blood!

Chapter 5

I scrambled from under my plant protection and grabbed Josh's antenna. His lithe body was now mush, but I pulled him toward me and cradled his jumbled parts. My poor Josh. It was all my fault.

My body felt numb, pain jutted to all extremities, much like when I had a brain freeze from ice cream, though that was more centralized, this more soul consuming. A lump grew in my thorax the size of a ten-carat diamond. Water leaked from all three of my eyes, dripping onto his still body.

He was too young to get a tree pot. He didn't know how to apply, he hadn't filled out the paperwork, filled out the duplicate copies, submitted it to the right departments.

We don't mourn the deceased on Zorca-twenty-three. We envy them. A tree pot is heaven for an ananoid. When you come from a crowded, rocky planet, the idea of your own coniferous tree abounding with berries, apples, melons, and every other fruit imaginable is Nirvana. But I didn't know what happened on Earth. I know you go to different places, depending on your religion, but all that totally confused me. And would Josh qualify for Earthling afterlife? Would your Higher Powers hold it against him if he's in insect form? I mean, we are known for our praying stance, which should account for something.

Plus, I really wasn't processing anything right now. Our future was stomped out in the step of a boot.

We'd had so many plans, Josh and I, so many places to cross off our bucket list. But now he'd kicked the bucket, and we hadn't even checked one thing off.

When I travelled through the black hole on my way to your planet, I must have developed Earth feelings, because I missed Josh. Big time. I missed him with my head, my heart, and my mandibles. He was one of a kind, and I would do whatever it took to make him whole again.

Even if it killed me.

Chapter 6

My eyes had never seeped like this before.

Josh couldn't be gone. We'd only had a short time together on your stupid planet. Life wasn't fair, and death was so one-sided and sucked even more.

I cradled him with my powerful front legs and used my back ones to open my *hanaglug*. Locating the *mist book*, I flipped through as vapors swirled around me, enveloping us in a hazy hug. Stars, although there were five pages of instructions on how to drive a car in London (fat lot of good that would do me) and the history of Rockhedge Circle (whatever that might be) and instructions for communicating with penguins—it definitely needed to be revised, and I'd complain to my handler Zen first thing when I got back home—the book had only one short paragraph on first aid.

Feel antennas. If warm, good. If cold, bad.

Who the heck wrote these stupid instructions? I tenderly wound my mandible around Josh's limp antenna. Arctic cold.

My one true love was gone. Sure, I'd had boyfriends before. It's not like I was totally a novice dater, but I hadn't had much luck in the love department. On Zorca-twenty-three I'd dated Fooonzy, who dated everything and anything with a pulse (and once without, if the rumors are to be believed). And then I moved on to Gorget and thought he was "the one." Well, when I told him I was leaving to visit Earth to bring home Ralb, he said I couldn't go. It's so not cool to have a mawl dictate what you can and cannot do. I broke up with him, and he wasted no time at all in dating my arch enemy, Kaj.

But Josh was different.

The entire time we were together I was the center of his universe, as he was mine. We were like seeds in a milk pod.

The first time I laid eyes on Josh, I was in human form, and he had the cutest tush of any mawl I'd ever seen. Not that I'm so superficial that was why I went out with him, but let's face it, it certainly helps if your mawl looks hot in jeans.

And now it was my entire dang fault he was dead. Deceased at seventeen. I rocked his corpse back and forth, and guilt seeped through me from my antenna to the tip of my walking legs.

If only he hadn't fallen in love with me, he wouldn't have taken the pill turning him into a praying mantis. Instead, he'd have been doing something nice and safe like playing NHL hockey or dismantling bombs.

Overhead, the bird's foot trefoil dipped closer.

John Stonegate reached past the plant and extended a hand. Two smelly feet landed on the platform right above us. "Look who we have here." John's announcer voice took on a desperate-to-catch-the crowd's-attention edge as people's attention drifted toward other passing celebrities. "The winner of Suzzy Newsworthy's *So You Wanna Be Me* contest—Ralb."

My brother's familiar, and majorly obnoxious, laugh rang in my ears.

My eyes were still dripping big time but seeing Ralb gave me an idea. An idea about how I could save Josh. I'd watched Zen reassemble other ananoids from miscellaneous parts. Maybe he could put Josh back together again.

I'd missed the contest part, but if Ralb had won, he'd take us along. Wouldn't he?

John Stonegate chuckled. "So, Ralb, are you a major superstar with only one name?"

"When you're as good as I am you only need one." Ralb slapped John Stonegate on the back, almost knocking the interviewer off the podium. "Only kidding, actually my real name is Bertie Star, but my friends call me Ralb, so that's what I go by now. Everyone is my friend."

Yes, my brother had reverted back to his Zorca-twenty-three name of Ralb. How typically arrogant, but then that's my brother for you. More importantly, though, I was interested to see if there were going to be major fireworks. Ralb and Suzz hadn't parted on the best of terms.

"Ralb, I'm so glad you won." Suzz leaned across John and air kissed Ralb's cheek. "The contest wasn't fixed, although Ralb and I do have some history together, and I for one will be delighted to finish what we started." She laughed and air kissed Ralb's date. "Nicola, how great to see you. Being at death's door seems to be a great way to lose that excess weight."

Was death knocking one more doors than Josh and mine? *Go away, death, go away.*

What the heck was my brother doing here? How had he managed to win the contest? Even more importantly, why was my BFF with him? Had she lost all her marbles in a casino?

Last time I'd seen Nicola, she was back in Bedrocktown, not feeling too well, the victim of the *E. coli* poisoning that had hit the town. I—not to pat myself on the back, which even I couldn't do while holding Josh—saved her life. Not to mention the lives of everyone in town. Not that I expect a statue or anything in my honor, though a parade would not go unappreciated, especially if I got to ride on one of those flowery floats.

And my brother! He should have been navigating us back home, not rubbing elbows (and other parts, if I knew him) with the rich and famous.

"Thank you, John." My brother instantly adopted the interviewee role. "Nicola and I are thrilled to be here, and I am more than excited to win the contest."

"Anyone who can answer Suzzy Newsworthy questions and get each one correct deserves to share the red carpet with the lady herself." John stepped back so all four of them were standing on the taped X.

"You know, sugar, I didn't know the answer to some of them myself." Suzzy giggled. "How did you know the name of my third-grade substitute teacher, the one who filled in when awful Ms. Renop went on maternity leave?"

"A simple matter of deduction, my dear," Ralb said like a movie detective.

I wouldn't have been at all surprised to see him don a floppy-eared hat and start smoking a pipe. To claim my brother is a drama queen would be like stating Hollywood has some bizarre dresses. Major understatement.

"I was determined to win and, if it meant searching

through grade school yearbooks, I was up to the task. My girl here is a huge Suzzy Newsworthy fan, and since it's my goal to keep her happy, I had to win the tickets."

All this fake happiness, all these plastic smiles were too much. I glanced down at Josh and gently rubbed his poor torn apart remains. My stomach felt as empty as my heart. Despite the fact it was stillthrobbing in my body, I wouldn't have been surprised to see my heart torn out and lying beside me on the red carpet. Despair filled me from my head down to the last inch of each mandible, but in spite of that, my insides felt hollow. Tears streamed from all three of my eyes as I tried to shelter Josh from drowning. Even though he was already deceased, I didn't want to kill him twice. I'm sure on Zorca-twenty-three we had tear ducts built in, but I'd never had the occasion to use them. I quietly hummed the first song that popped into my head. A song I constantly heard, a tune that never seems to leave your brain.

"If you stare up at a star

The star don't care who you are."

I repeated it my lucky seventeen times, but he still didn't move a muscle. He was gone. My reason for living, my, cute-tushed Josh was gone.

I caused his demise, so it was up to me to save him. I couldn't sit here all day beside the planter wishing things were different. There's an old saying on Zorca-twenty-three. *If wishes were spaceships, poor aliens would fly*. I had to help Josh.

I was smart, I was intelligent. I was a femawl. I could help Josh. And dang it, I would.

Maybe the *mist book* had resuscitation directions. I

turned the pages so feverishly the breeze ruffled the overhead flowers. There had to be something in here to help. Please tell me it wasn't a useless book I'd been hauling around, giving me muscles I didn't want.

Finally, I got to the section I needed:

If your demise occurs on earth, all is not lost. You must return to Zorca-twenty-three within two days and get a shot of Remmo. (These instructions brought to you by the fine ananoids at Remmo, Inc.) The instructions didn't explain how to get back to Zorca-twenty-three if you were deceased, but luckily Josh had me to help.

Yes! There was a way to save Josh. I hugged him tighter, a little too close apparently as a little of his insides oozed out. If Zen couldn't do it, Remmo could. But I had to get Josh aboard that spaceship. Now. How the heck could I get self-centered Ralb to notice us?

"Aww, isn't he the sweetest?" Nicola's giggle attracted my attention as she squeezed Ralb's arm.

What? When the heck did that happen? Last I remembered, Ralb was kissing Suzz, and Nicola was sick in bed. I had a major brain clog from then till now.

Gosh, how long had I been out of it?

I peeked around to see Suzz's expression. If a person could turn green with envy, well, that was our gal. To be honest, the thought of Ralb being with anyone I knew was enough to upset my innards.

I'd better stop carpet dreaming and listen up. Then I might learn what on earth—and other places—my BFF saw in my brother, and more importantly find a way to help my Josh.

Nicola stepped closer to the mic. "Suzzy Newsworthy. She's the best, and it was so nice to have her give me a dress from her clothing line, Dark Ally."

From underneath my shelter, I watched my BFF smooth down a moth-eaten dress. It had more holes than the ozone layer, and most were not strategically placed. The color could best be described as barf, and that was totally not in Nicola's color palette.

"Ralb offered me his seat on the spaceship," Nicola said, "but I'm afraid of heights, so this was a nice consolation prize, meeting all the celebrities and especially you, John."

"And what a fashion statement you're making"— John flicked the dandelion in my brother's pocket, and Ralb cringed— "to wear a wilting sunflower, one which obviously has seen better days."

"That's got to go," Suzzy Newsworthy ordered. "I hate weeds."

"Right." Ralb tossed the dandelion onto the floor, mere centimeters from where we were huddled.

Stars above, he'd be in trouble. Big time. That wasn't a mere dandelion or sunflower. It was Rotsen. No one tossed Rotsen around like he was yesterday's newspaper. Rotsen is from Zorca-twenty-three, a Soprano-quoting-from-the television-show dandelion, and you definitely don't want to get on the wrong side of him. Someone majorly ticked him off on Zorca-twenty-three, and last I heard that someone was still circling space on an asteroid, counterclockwise.

"Who you calling wilting, you moron? I'm a dandelion, not a sunflower. Cripes, I oughta rub you out, just on that alone." Rotsen pointed a leaf toward John Stonegate, and the leaf took on the shape of a gun. Only Zorcans could hear his threat, but still I feared for the announcer. I wasn't a fan of Stonegate's journalism, but no one deserved to be given attitude by a dandelion.

Stars know, I'd had enough of Rotsen's arrogance to last several lifetimes. It even quadtroupled Ralb's.

"Rotsen, it's me," I telepathed him. He had to help Josh and me, even if it was to make burial arrangements. No doubt if I had to rely on Ralb, we'd be trampled like the people in those bullfights. I might as well have been waving a red cape at those stilettos.

"Quit playing with me. You're nowhere near here." Rotsen cranked his head around, presumably in search of us, but he looked like one of those battery-powered plastic flowers that danced to annoying songs. "Now, more importantly, where did our little Suzzy Newsworthy go? Did you know she was totally checking me out? I must admit she was undressing me with her eyes. She totally thinks I'm a hunkarama."

"You know she's Suzz, right? The Suzz we last saw on her dad's farm of SplinterRock who dissed me."

"No way," Rotsen answered. "No way would Suzz check me out, and besides Suzzy Newsworthy has purple hair and Suzz did not." He paused. "So, you're definitely wrong-o."

I wanted to say, "Rotsen, get over yourself. You're a dandelion with a major attitude," but I needed his help badly, so I bit my tongue and instead kissed his petals. "Rotsen, if she had half a brain in her head, she'd be snuggling up to you big time. But right now, Josh and I need your help. He's in no shape to help himself, and we have to get out of here."

"What's wrong, Oas? Why do you look like yesterday's dinner? A right old bag of hammers? You really need to use some of Suzzy Newsworthy's makeup. Your face looks horrid."

"Thanks for the compliments." I took a deep

breath. "Josh is dead." Geez, is it any wonder I looked like crap with a ten-ton meteor crushing on my heart? I gently stroked his head and cradled his mangled body.

Rotsen glanced over at us and cringed. "What did you do to him? He's flatter than a piece of shale."

Flabbergasted, I shook my mandible at him. "How could you think I'd do something like this to him? I love him, loved him, er, love him."

"You have a funny way of showing it. I hope you don't love me." Rotsen took a step back, out of swatting distance.

"Shut up and listen. I have a plan to save him."

"Sweetheart, the only plan you should be making is how deep to bury him."

"You're mean." I patted what was once Josh's head. "Fine, I'll do it alone. I don't need your help. When have you ever helped me? You're as bad as Ralb. Nothing but a major pain in the thorax."

"Hey, calm down now. You had to know I was just joshing, er, maybe that wasn't the best choice of words. What's your plan? I know it'll be good. Your ideas always are." He smoothed down his top petal and stood up ramrod straight. "Hit me with your best shot."

"Rotsen, if I can just get him home, back to Zorca-twenty-three, Zen can help us. He can save Josh. If Zen can't reassemble Josh, there's this shot called *Remmo* that might work." Ignoring Rotsen's it's-never-going-to-happen face, I rushed to explain. "All I have to do is get us on SpaceMoonOne, jump onto the Space Port, hop over to a passing meteorite in Zorca-twenty-three's atmosphere, and then find a way to get from there to Zorca." I took a breath. I hadn't mentioned the toughest part. "And we have two days to do it." *Easy as an alien landing in Area fifty-one, right?*

"I guess you don't want me to tell you that plan has more holes than Earthen Swiss Cheese."

"No, I don't. If you don't have anything positive to say, then keep your petals shut." I stood, almost forgetting I had Josh in my lap. Just in time, I grabbed his parts to keep them from hitting the red carpet. "Come full or crescent moon, I'll get Josh home, and I will find a way to make him better, with or without your help."

"You only have two days, or Zen can't do nada for your mawlfriend, *capisce*?" Rotsen took on the know-it-all tone I detested.

"I know. That's why I'm getting on Suzzy Newsworthy's ship."

"You do know it's leaving in two hours?" He folded his leaves and adopted a cocky stance.

"Rotsen, I'm warning you. Either be with me or without me, but I'm saving Josh's life. Whatever it takes."

"What are you going to do? Suck up to Suzzy Newsworthy? That's your plan? Don't you think she'll be able to see through you like a telescope?"

I wrapped my arms around Josh again. "If need be, I'll do whatever sucking up is needed. But first I'll talk to her, make her see reason. I'll remind her of our friendship. She liked Ralb at one point, that's got to account for something."

"This should be good."

Chapter 7

"You've got bigger problems." Rotsen whispered. "Kaj is on her way here."

"What? Tell me you're lying!" I croaked. If Suzzy Newsworthy was my worst enemy on Earth, Kaj held that position on Zorca-twenty-three. She stole Gorget from me, okay I was finished with him, but I would have liked for him to have a period of mourning before she warmed his antennas.

He shrugged his leaves and shook his petals. "My sources are reliable."

"I'll be long gone before she sets her size twelve foot on this planet." All the more reason for me to get my butt in gear and get Josh back to Zorca-twenty-three. "Come on, *tempis fugit*, we have to get Josh home."

"I'll do what I can. I'll telepath Ralb right now so we can get this action-packed plan into play." Rotsen stood at attention, seriousness taking over his usual playful demeanor.

In a manner of minutes, my bro was standing in front of us. He bent over and picked up Rotsen, smoothing down his petals and leaves in a fashion that reminded me of a caring Parental Being, not like mine who had more than six hundred offspring. Ralb was smart enough to know he was in big-time trouble.

"Ralb, your sister is here too," Rotsen telepathed.

"What the frig is she doing here?" Ralb whispered out of the corner of his mouth. He glanced around. "Rotsen, are you messing with me? I don't see her."

"We're down here, between the plants in the container with the TZZ logo on the ground."

Cripes, Rotsen needed a GPS, because with the instructions he gave to Ralb, my brother couldn't find us.

"Come on, Ralb, quit with the slo-mo actions. Josh is badly hurt, and I need to get him fixed up." I hated to ask Ralb for favors because it would come back to bite me big time in my lower extremities, but I had to do it for Josh. "Ralb, I'm warning you. Pick us up right now or I'll…"

"Sorry, Oas can't hear you." Ralb strolled away.

I wished I had a skipping stone to lob at his retreating back. I'm not a violent person, but I'd go to jail if it meant that Josh could live. *Please, whatever Superior Being might be listening, I'll make any deal you want if Josh survives.*

Why wouldn't Ralb help us?

I was forced to face the sad truth. My annoying sibling was going to leave me and Josh on the carpet to dart high heels like we were in a stupid video game.

I'd talk to Suzz. Beg if I had to. I had to get Josh to Zorca-twenty-three. If she wouldn't help, I'd take matters into my own two antennas.

To implement Project Josh, I checked out the lowest shoes, ones we could hitch a ride on. Strappy sandals strolled by some with fringe, others with beads, a few with jewels. Men's shoes would be easier to stick to. If I could just hang onto one tassel, we should be GtoG.

Stars! Where was a tassel when I needed one?

Suddenly, a hand swiped down between the fronds of the palms. I closed my eyes, afraid I'd met my demise. I'd lived a good life, alas not long enough, but the years I did live were pretty exciting. I'd traveled to Earth, eaten ice cream, and gotten a brain freeze. I'd also tried popcorn and pizza, both with disastrous results, but, hey, I live to learn. I peeled open one eye, then the second, and finally the third.

I screamed.

It wasn't Ralb who'd scooped us up, but someone much worse.

Chapter 8

"John Stonegate, I told you that flowerpot was in the wrong spot. You're going to have to move it," a firm voice called out. "The camera keeps picking up that off-color palm leaf, and the green is throwing off the entire shot." A hairy arm reached beneath the planter rim and scraped us up off the cushy carpet. I clutched tightly to Josh, not wanting him to fall from the great heights where we were dangling.

John flipped a button on the box on his waist to ensure his mike was off and glared at the camerawoman. "Marlene, I'll move it, okay? Don't get your g-string in a twist." Muttering to himself, he said, "Better get rid of these bugs too. Geez, talk about cutbacks. One minute interviewing Suzzy Newsworthy, the next, I'm a friggin' garbage man."

He gathered us both in a tissue smelling of Suzzy Newsworthy's perfume, no doubt one of the escapees from her breast stuffing. He stalked across the carpet and dumped us into an ashtray filled with sand and cigarette butts. With as much energy as I could muster, I pulled myself up to the silver lip. Just then, an empty gum package landed in the ashtray, hitting my torso, and ricocheting my *hanaglug* along with us out the side. I grabbed on with one antenna so we didn't free-fall to the carpet.

The interviewer brushed off his hands and strode

41

Jane Greenhill

over to Ralb. He motioned toward the nearest cameraman. "He's got his sights on our little Suzzy Newsworthy. Can you imagine waking up next to her? You'd be in a coyote situation there. You'd want to bite your arm off so you wouldn't wake her up and have to listen to those stupid sayings."

"I know her from way back," Ralb bragged. "I used to be her boyfriend."

"Any secrets you'd like to share with us, off the record?" John asked companionably. "I won't say where I got the scoop, but, hey, if it pans out, it could be very—and I mean very—lucrative for you."

"Well, she likes to—"

"Ralb, Oas is in trouble." Rotsen and I were on the same frequency.

I clung by my antenna to the side of the ashtray six feet off the ground, Josh wrapped tightly in my mandible. I was reluctant to have to rely on my brother to save us. I'd never hear the end of it—again. Like a mountain climber, I pulled us up over the side. We crash landed into a vat of sand. My *hanaglug* landed alongside, setting off a sandstorm.

"She's always trouble," Ralb muttered. He pocketed John Stonegate's business card as the announcer made the universal "call me" sign.

John Stonegate made sure he'd flipped his microphone off. "Women usually are," he muttered. "She's a real handful."

"You don't know the half of it," Ralb agreed. "Sisters, can't live with them, can't kill them off without upsetting your parents."

"I didn't know Suzzy Newsworthy was your sister." The announcer crossed his arms. "I don't think

42

family members are allowed to enter the contest."

"She's not my sister." Ralb's two eyes bulged in their sockets. "It's bad enough I have the ones I do. I don't need one like Suzzy."

John Stonegate leaned closer, an eager expression on his face. "Who were you talking about then?"

Seeming to realize he was talking himself into a deep hole, Ralb shrugged. "No one you'd know."

"So, tell me about Suzzy."

"Where to begin?" Ralb snuggled closer to Nicola. "Honey, he wants details about Suzz."

Nicola rolled her eyes Zorca-twenty-three ward. "Suzz sure has changed since we knew her," Nicola said. "We used to be BFFs. Now she doesn't have the time of day for either of us."

"I hope you never change, babe."

"Why would I do that?" She leaned her head against his chest and gaze into his eyes. "You're too cute."

Aww, geez, can someone find me a spoon to stop my gagging? I can't take much more of the mushiness. Major grossness. My stomach contents couldn't handle any more. I would soon be exporting major mantis puke.

How unfair life was. Here I sat in a sandy, smelly ashtray, dodging burning projectiles like I was in a war-torn country, while my bro chatted up movie stars.

I threw one butt back at the actor who was in that awful musical. My Josh didn't need third degree burns on top of his other problems. Really, does it take that much effort to show a little respect? I'm just saying, next time you throw something in the trash, take a gander and make sure there's no one in there who might get hurt.

I rubbed Josh's antenna, feeling a tad hopeful as it felt a little warmer than before, but maybe that was from the heat of the cigarette butts. My lungs filled with the noxious smoke. Being trapped in a forest fire couldn't be worse. For a moment, I was glad Josh wasn't breathing. He didn't need a disease too.

John headed back toward the ashtray, motioning toward the camerawoman. "Could you tell me where you'd like the stupid plant once and for all?" He smirked and added to Ralb and Nicola, "Marlene's upset because Martin invited me to his private after party at Spragot and didn't invite her. Sucks to be her."

"Martin invited you to a party?" Even from my precarious position, the awe in Nicola's voice was unmistakable.

"Yep. You want to come? I can round up another ticket." He glanced toward Ralb. "It would be completely platonic. I'd treat her like she was my sister."

Man above, I hope he cares for his family better than Ralb cares for his own.

"John, are you serious?" Nicola screamed like she was at a Smith Brothers concert. I covered my ears with my mandibles. How nice to see that the death of my recently murdered mawl, resting in a pit of smelly cigarette, cigar, and quite a few "herbal" butts, wouldn't stand in the way of a good night out.

"Sure. Just find me after the show, and I'll hook you up." He glanced over Ralb's shoulder and raised his arm, snapping his fingers. "Julia, over here."

He strong-armed Ralb out of the way, and my wimp of a brother grimaced. I hoped John had shoved him in the same place where Nicola elbowed him.

"Ralb, we have to help Oas," Rotsen said in a stage whisper. "Some things are more important than your social life. If the situation were reversed, Oas would be the first one to help you out."

"We don't know where she is, so there's really no rush to find her. Why don't we enjoy the party, then look into finding her?" He glanced in the direction of Milley Venture. "It's not like she's going anywhere and, besides, this is a once in a lifetime opportunity." He hip-joined to Nicola, and my already queasy stomach somersaulted. I could not have my BFF hooking up with my bratty brother. That would throw the constellations out of orbit.

"I can't believe April is missing this. Where is she?" Nicola asked, apparently not upset by the closeness of my brother's hand to her behind.

Then my smooth operator brother rubbed her earlobe. When we get out of the mess we're in, or rather out of the sandpit ashtray, I was so going to have to speak to her and shake some sense into her. What was she thinking? Obviously, nothing at all.

Would she really want to kiss lips that had touched Suzz's?

Nicola is a human, and when I switched back into my Zorca-twenty-three form, she'd been sick in bed. She had no idea that Ralb and I were aliens, but to be honest, if Josh (may he rest in peace) was okay with it, Nicola probably would be too. If I could ever get out of this smoker's tar pit.

"Fine. Any idea where the little drama queen might be?" Ralb was talking into the flower like it was a listening device in a spy show. Rotsen wouldn't be impressed. He was a one-woman dandelion. And even when he gave me major attitude, he always had my back.

"You kids slay me. You're all going to owe me big time, and I mean to collect," Rotsen ranted in his best New Jersey mobster accent he'd learnt from way too many movies. "Even if I have to break your kneecaps or put you in cement shoes, I'll collect. I'll—"

"Geez, Rotsen, if it wasn't for us, you'd still be stuck on Zorca-twenty-three listening to Xron go on about his tree pot," Ralb said. "You should be thanking us for giving you an adventure, not threatening us."

"Fine, whatev." Rotsen rubbed his dandelion petals across Ralb's face. "If you can get your head out of the stars long enough, you'd realize she's right behind you in the ashtray." He laughed. "Not that I don't think she belongs in the garbage, but even she shouldn't have to put up with wads of chewed up gum." He paused. "Just a thought, though. If we can figure out whose gum it is, we might be able to put it on the Internet and make a fortune."

"Oh gosh, Ralb. Look! It's Virgin." Nicola screamed. "Tonight keeps on getting better and better." She jumped up and kissed Ralb on the cheek. "Oh wait, Suzzy Newsworthy is sucking up to Justin Squirrel." Nicola emitted a high-pitched screech that I'm sure had dogs in the area covering their ears. She waved at Suzzy Newsworthy. A few seconds later, her hand dropped to her side. "Would you look at her? She's pretending she doesn't even know me."

"Don't worry. You know what she's like." Ralb reached out to shake hands with one of the Creek cast members, who raised his eyebrows but accepted the hand.

"Hello, over there." I telepathed to Ralb. "*Tempis fugit* and all. You might have all the time in the world to schmooze with the rich and famous, but I have a spaceship to catch." How would he feel if the situation were reversed, and I was the one in control?

"Calm down, sis."

When someone tells you to calm down, doesn't it make you want to throttle them? Come closer, bro, and feel the wrath of my jackknife legs. I'll show you a scissor kick you won't soon forget.

"I have everything under control. I'm on my way to speak to Suzz and ask if you can join us." He turned to slap the back of the Hottest Man of the Year, at least according to *Persone* magazine. Obviously they'd never seen my Josh.

"Rotsen," I telepathed, "Suzz-slash-Suzzy Newsworthy has seen me in my true form. What if she spills the beans about me and Ralb?"

"No worries, my little shish kabob," he said. "When we left SplinterRock, the double lightning bolts that hit the silo caused a major blackout in the town and temporarily gave everyone a senior moment." He arched his stem. "Because of her close proximity to the silo, her brain got a tad fried, so she can't remember anything or anyone from that night, other than it caused her to become an unbelievable singer." He brushed aside one of his petals. "Speaking of Little Miss Famous, where did she learn those moves?"

I followed his line of sight. Our little farm girl was tripping the light fantastic with the latest celebrity dancing competition winner, cameras flashing in time to their steps. Suzzy twirled out before gliding back and floating into the arms of her dancing partner, her penguin feathers floating like dandelion fluff. Every cameraman in sight dropped his equipment and clapped madly. Grinning like the Cheshire cat she was, she two-stepped toward her partner. Flushed and laughing, she popped a piece of gum into her mouth, chewed quickly, and then kissed her dancing partner on the lips.

Oh no, I knew what that gleam in her eyes meant. Our Suzzy Newsworthy was up to no good. She was like an addict, zeroing in on another celebrity, waiting for the next hit.

Then even worse than John Stonegate's ugly hairy hands tossing Josh and me into our pit of despair, Suzzy Newsworthy strolled beside our prison, waving and blowing kisses to her fans. She tossed her hunk of chewed-up gum in our vicinity.

I inhaled.

And choked.

Cripes, out of all the flavors of gum, why did she have to choose popcorn? Popped corn and I do not mix. We're like garlic and jellybeans. Who in their right mind would come up with that combination? Personally, I bet whoever did is now selling newspapers in Alaska in the middle of winter. But then, maybe it's a great way to protect yourself from vampires.

"Ralb, uh, Ralb. Get over there, ASAP," Rotsen telepathed. "Oas needs your help. Big time."

"Yeah, yeah, yeah. How many times have I heard that in my life? Ralb, Oas needs you." He nuzzled closer to Nicola. "Nicola and I are heading inside. We'll deal with my sister later."

In a voice that didn't bear argument, my now-favorite dandelion mind-warped orders to Ralb. "She's in that silver cylinder. Go and pick her out of the trash. Then you can party till you're pumpernickel for all I care."

"Nic, can you hang tight for a minute? I have a tissue that I need to dispose of." He pecked my BFF on the cheek and then headed toward us.

I'm so going to tell Nicola what a jerk he is as soon as he rescues me.

"Rotsen, I don't know what you're talking about." Ralb smirked down at me. "All I see here is some squished up bug covered with butts."

"Ralb, if you don't get us out of here, I'm going to—"

"Oas, is that you?" He reached down and scooped us up in the tissue he was pretending to dispose of. I grabbed my *hanaglug*. "Please don't mind your mode of transportation, but I used this to wipe bug splat off the windshield of my car." He smirked. "I guess you'll be right at home with bug carcasses, though."

"Ralb, you have the same DNA I do."

"That may be true, dear sister, but I'm here in human form mixing with the rich and famous. Yes, I'm hanging with one of the hottest entertainment reporters, whereas you, my dear, are mixing it up with Rotsen and the lapel of my jacket." He laughed. "It must suck to be you."

"You are such a dolt." I couldn't wrap my head around the fact that he was here with Nicola, much less that I had to rely on him to save my cute little tush. "Did you really have to ignore Rotsen for so long?"

If I'd had the energy and was slightly bigger, I would have smacked him. Just wait until I'm up and about and not in mourning, because he was a major goner. But unlike my poor Josh, I so wouldn't be giving him any *Remmo*. I poked my head out from the top of the tissue. At least I could breathe Earth oxygen, instead of cigarette smoke.

"And how would you like to be put back with the trash?" He made a move as if to toss the tissue into the bin. I screamed like the femawl I am. "Ralb, I'm sorry." I crossed my antennas behind my head so he couldn't see. "I'll never annoy you again."

"Really, you mean you're not going to bug me?" He squeezed me a little too hard. "Get it, bug me." He lifted us toward Rotsen so I could scoot us out onto a dandelion petal.

"Hey, sweetheart, no need to get mushy." Rotsen tucked us under his left leaf so we were cushioned between it and Ralb's suit jacket.

"Ralb, what on earth were you doing with those bugs?" Nicola asked, obviously not knowing it was her BFF she was criticizing. "Would you like me to toss them for you? It looks like a huge hunk of dandruff, and you want to be pristine when we meet Simone."

"You're so right, my little baby-boo. But I'll just be a sec."

She squeezed Ralb's arm. "I still can't believe we're going to a party with Martin. I wish more than anything that April could be here with us."

"She is." Ralb caressed her hand, and I reached around Rotsen to poke him with my antenna.

"Let him talk," Rotsen said. "Maybe it's time she knows."

"What do you mean she's here?" Nicola's head snapped around like she was in that movie *The Txxorcist*, only without the vomiting. One of the perils of too much exercise, I guess.

"Nicola, there's something you should know." Ralb tucked a loose strand of hair behind her ear. Even from my vantage point, major bling twinkled in her ears, brighter than the North Star.

"Oh my God, there's Joe Smith." She smoothed down her dress. "I wonder if he's sitting near us." Obviously my BFF was forgetting about me, now that one of the Brothers was in the vicinity. "Come on, Ralb, let's find our seats. I'm sure April will catch up to us sooner or later." She tugged his arm so hard that I almost lost my grip on his jacket. My head swung one way, my body, the other. Man alive, she was acting like Suzz around a boy. Granted Joe was a cutie, but I'm the BFF who nursed her back to health. Well, maybe her mom did most of the work, but I was in the general area. Just goes to show you when a mawl enters the picture and a rich mawl at that—not to say that Nic is superficial or anything—well, BFFs fly right out the window.

"I'm sure April will track us down, and really why should we ruin our night waiting for her to come out of the woodwork?" Ralb swatted at Rotsen.

I was so going to get him rubbed out, and I don't mean on a chalkboard.

Rotsen stroked my head, trying to calm me down, but really just pushing Josh and me closer to Suzzy's discarded gum. It stuck to my *hanaglug,* but I'd worry about it later. Once I got him to stop shoving us into the gum, I promised Rotsen I wouldn't do anything rash. Eventually I'd give my brother the biggest wedgie he'd ever had, but in the meantime, I was going to remain calm, cool, and calculating.

Remember Josh! Remember Josh! Before all else I had to protect Josh and get him back home.

"Josh," I whispered. "You will make it. Together we will venture to my universe, and once again you will be whole, cute tush and all. Together we will conquer the cosmos."

Around us slot machines rang out, their chimes accented by the sounds of coins hitting the metal trays, the noise rousing Rotsen enough that he poked his head out beside me. We had the best vantage point in the world as Ralb and Nic walked into the theater.

Rotsen's eyes were the size of the coins falling from the machines. "Baby, this is Vegas! Long Live Las Vegas." He squealed. Rubbing his leaves together, he continued. "Bring it on baby."

Geez, didn't I have enough to worry about with Josh. Now I'd have to keep an eye on Rotsen and make sure he didn't end up with a gambling addiction.

"You got to know when to hang on ta yor cards, hang on ta yor cards." Thankfully, he didn't sing the rest, though his out of tune humming was equally annoying.

I tried to pay no mind to him and instead turned to take in the sights.

Ashtrays squatted beside overweight patrons who looked like they knew the locations of all the buffets. I shifted my line of sight. If I never saw another ashtray again, it would be too soon. I'd enjoy this show a lot more with Josh by my side. All three of my eyes began to leak. Our eyes on Zorca-twenty-three never water, so I don't know where the liquid came from. And a lump formed in my thorax the size of meteorite. I missed Josh. He always had my back even when he was looking at my front.

Gently I stroked my poor, deceased mawlfriend's face. He had a hunk of Suzzy's gum stuck to the side of his head. We'd be able to remove it with the trusty ice cube trick. I certainly didn't want him buried with her DNA. That would be, to me, the final insult.

With the skill of a plastic surgeon, I used my thumb and index finger to pull the wad off him. Salty fumes overcame me. My leg tingled. My arm shook. I tried not to inhale, but I almost suffocated. It couldn't be happening. Salt caused me—and Josh—to change from humanoid to alien. Popcorn had salt. Table salt was bad enough. My brother had thrown table salt on Josh, and I had reverted back to my Zorca-twenty-three praying mantis status, but gritty sea salt had to be a hundred times worse.

I changed from ananoid to humanoid when I travelled here through the Black Hole, but since I was now an ananoid the salt was having the opposite effect.

Oh stars! Heavens above. What the heck was I going to do?

I was morphing into a humanoid in my brother's pocket.

Chapter 9

Cramps knotted my stomach. They were ten times worse than the last time I morphed. My neck muscles wrenched, my head twisting and turning as my chromosomes altered.

My upper regions transformed first, and surprisingly the multimillion-dollar-paycheck stars didn't bat an eye when Ralb looked like he had two heads.

With grace I didn't know he possessed, Ralb slid behind a three-meter-high brass urn filled with foliage in the colors of TZZ.

"Nicola, would you mind getting me a program?" He pointed to the usher dressed in red with a small pillbox hat on his head. "I want to remember this night forever."

"Great idea," she said without looking over at us. "Maybe I can suck up to him and get two."

Ralb helped me out of his pocket. My walking sticks, I mean, my legs, stretched out until I was standing beside Ralb, who had the good sense to lean over, sheltering me from the public. My mandibles immediately flew to my head. Hey, I'd been a humanoid before, so I knew how important a good hair style was. My fingers hit curls, lots of curls. I pulled one, and it sprang right back. I checked my reflection in the brass urn. Great, I had the hair of those Irish dancers. Shapeshifting made me dizzy. My heels were so high, I teetered like I was about to fall off a balance beam. I was definitely a fashion victim, but major lucky I shifted fully clothed. There was a story going around Zorca-twenty-three about one of the earlier Earth travels where the change took place and the Zorcan ended up naked in the middle of a circus. Well, the audience hardly noticed because of the skimpy costumes, but the elephants had a heyday.

Cameras and flashes went off. I sucked in my stomach and stood as tall as I could. Autograph hounds jostled and nudged each other to get the best view of the celebrities. Thank God, Nicola was too caught up with the uproar of the crowds to be concerned about what Ralb was doing. Maybe there was hope for her yet.

I stretched my sore neck and rounded my shoulders trying to work out the cramps. My body ached like I'd been wedged in a clown car with a large rubber foot jabbed into my *esophagut*.

Then reality hit me.

If I was changing into a human, Josh would be too.

My beloved would evolve back into the mawl I loved. Once again I'd gaze deeply into his eyes, losing myself in those brown orbs the color of tree trunks. I'd get to check out his butt, which believe me is almost as fine as his face. I'd have his hand intertwined through mine, and he'd caress my palm in that special way that sent shivers through my torso. I'd feel his kissable lips against mine, his tongue venturing into my mouth and not in a totally gross way. I'd definitely lucked out with my first Earth mawlfriend.

Eek! What was I thinking? How was I going to

manage to hide a mangled, dead body? It wasn't like I could tuck him under my arm and pretend he wasn't there.

Wait. How long had the gum been stuck to him before I noticed? He hadn't altered. Was it because he was extinguished like the butts we had so recently kept company with? But how was I going to preserve him?

Stars, what was I going to do?

Think, Oas, think.

I opened my *mist book* and laid his limp body inside. What happens in the *mist book*, stays in the *mist book*. He would be safe and sound in there until I could get him the first aid he needed. Now I can see you shudder; obviously you've pressed flowers and bugs in your lifetime, and I'm not going to pass judgment on the bug part, but rest assured, Josh wouldn't get flattened any more than he already was.

I stared down at his remains, biting my lip to prevent myself from crying. I don't know how much water was in my system, but it seemed like it could fill a lake. I gently fingered Josh's antenna, remembering how we used to intertwine. I ran my hand over his mushed torso and picked the sticky gum from his antennas. I managed to remove it from his body without tearing any of his limbs.

That is, until Ralb hit my arm and I pulled off a major part of Josh's torso that every mawl needs.

Chapter 10

"Ralb, you're an idiot." Both of my hands held parts of Josh. I wasn't good at puzzles. I hated anything with parts that didn't fit together.

"April, where did you come from?" Nicola headed toward us.

I snapped the *mist book* shut, slid it into my bug-sized *hanaglug*, tucked them both in the tight pocket of my skirt, and stumbled toward her.

With two programs tucked under her arm and balancing crystal glasses in her left hand, Nicola gave me a one-armed hug with her right. "If I'd known you were coming, I would have gotten you a program." She laughed. "Look what else I got. Two goblets filled with Suzz's—er, I mean Suzzy Newsworthy's gum. Wonder what that will fetch me at home? I could raffle them off at the fair and raise money for the new hospital." She stopped and took a breath. "And where did you get the idea to wear those clothes? I love your hair, how cool going from straight blonde to red curls."

Panicked, I glanced down at a black sequined top and miniskirt. And somewhere in my travels, I'd had a pedicure; each toe was decorated with tiny petal-like dandelions. Rotsen must have had something to do with it, but for once I was glad for my bossy, narcissistic friend.

I moaned when she gripped my arm tightly. Her

fingernails dug into my skin. At this rate my BFF was going to kill me. I tried not to wince as I rubbed my arm to regain my circulation. "Maybe we should go."

"Ralb, can you believe your sister? She wants to leave."

I moved into a karate stance in case she tried to grab my arm again, but luckily she went for Ralb instead. I owed him one or maybe even two.

"Look, there's Jay Genuflect, Nic, and he looks like he wants to say *hi*." I pointed in one direction while I pulled Ralb in the other. Standing beside the garbage can dressed up to look like a golden statue, I yanked on his ear until it was beside my mouth. "Okay, did you hear Suzzy Newsworthy? She's heading up on the SpaceMoonOne. Do you know what that means?"

Rotsen lifted his head. "There's going to be one less hot chick on Earth?"

"More like one less airhead on this planet." I gritted my relatively new teeth. What is it about the mawl species, whether animal, mineral, or plant? They see a pretty girl, and it doesn't matter that there's nothing between her ears. I wish they'd think with their brains instead of their...well, you know what. It certainly makes life difficult for us smart girls.

"I see what you're saying." Ralb kept checking out the backs of the passing femawls. "Looks like we have a ride to hitch."

"Totally in agreement for once in our life, but I have to get up there sooner rather than later." I pawed at his arm. "I have to get Josh to Zen so we can bring him back to life."

Josh, who was no longer with us.

Tears welled, and I bit my lip to stop myself from

crying.

Big time sniffles. Snot dripped out of my nose like a torrential tropical rain.

Great!

The ultimate celebrity couple passed by arms entwined around each other. And here I was without my guy.

I cried for when I was part of a pair. I cried for the future I didn't have any more.

"I'm really sorry about this." Ralb pulled a handkerchief out of his pocket. What was it with him? Was he a circus clown with an endless supply of handkerchiefs attached to each other, each in different colors?

I wept harder.

I just wanted to go home.

My home.

It might be a rain-starved planet, but it was beautiful. Its three moons cast amazing hues on the limestone rocks no matter what the time of day. Tiny brush and cactus sprang from the cracks in the rocks, softening the rough edges.

I must have said that out loud, because Rotsen's sigh could, I'm sure, be heard in this galaxy and the next as well.

"Are you never happy?" he asked. "When you were on Zorca-twenty-three all you thought about was traveling to Earth to try pizza and soda. Now all you want to do is go back home." He flicked his leaf. "I really don't know what to do with you. You're fickle."

"But I have to get back for Josh," I said weakly.

"That and you're homesick. But, sweetheart, you better think up another plan quickly because Suzz is not about to let you share her spaceship."

Rotsen was right.

Ralb already had a seat lined up with his name on it, but I didn't. And now that I was in human shape, I couldn't hide out in his pocket. Unless I wanted to hang onto the side of the rocket like a barnacle on a ship, I'd have to finagle myself a seat.

I'd stage an acting job that would put Suzzy Newsworthy to shame. I had to face the lizard in her lair, battle the shark in high seas—so to speak, of course.

Shouldn't be too hard.

Asocar, look out.

Chapter 11

Maybe Ralb could convince her. I sidled over to my brother. "Did you talk to her?"

"I've been kind of busy, what with you shape shifting and all, but hang on." He yelled across the aisle. "Hey, Suzzy, can my sister come with us?"

"Over my dead body." Then she seemed to remember where she was and resumed her high-wattage grin. "There's no room, though maybe if she lost a stone or two." She turned her back on us.

"Well, I tried." He shrugged his bony shoulders and then turned *his* back on me.

I flipped him back around so he was facing me. I so wasn't putting up with his attitude today. Josh was dead, and I would kiss up to anyone and everyone if it meant he would be resurrected. I swallowed the lump in my throat and patted lovingly where Josh's corpse rested in I hoped peace. I would say goodbye, farewell to my man if it would save his life. "Ralb, will you take Josh back to Zorca-twenty-three and get him to Zen?"

He paused, rubbing the fur growing on his face. "I'm not going back home, Suzzy's asked me to act in her next project. Sis, I'm going to be a star."

Great, once again my brother was thinking of no one but himself. I'd like to make him see stars. There had to be another way for me to get home, to get Josh well again. I didn't need my useless brother's assistance.

Rotsen poked his head out, and then obviously not liking the drama went back into hiding. Great! When a dandelion doesn't have your back, you're in rough shape. Coward!

I bit my newly formed bottom lip and took a deep breath. It's for Josh, it's for Josh, I reminded myself. I would walk across hot coals for my man, and frankly I'd rather do that than have to ask *her* for any favors. But I had to do what I had to do.

"Suzzy, do you have a sec?" I pulled at her arm to get her attention, but she shrugged me off like I was yesterday's news. "I have to say; whoever did *your* lips did an amazing job. And your boobs are the best-looking ones here." I had to defrost the freezer, and if it took complimenting the Ice Queen to get Josh to Zorca-twenty-three, heck, I would. "They defy gravity."

"Can't you see I'm busy?" Suzzy fluffed her hair, pursed her lips, and stuck out her boobs so far she almost took my eyes out. "Yoohoo, Kimty over here."

Okay, it appeared flattery wouldn't work. I went in for the kill, so to speak. I took a step closer. "Suzz," I whispered, emphasizing the name to remind her I knew her past. A little blackmail might do what compliments couldn't. "I wouldn't bother you if it wasn't important. It's a matter of life and death."

"Geez, everything is always so dramatic with you." She looked me over from head to toe, and from the sour expression on her face she wasn't pleased with what she saw. Then with a sigh so deep I'm sure my Parental Beings heard it on Zorca-twenty-three, she said, "What is it?"

"Can we go somewhere private?" I asked. How

could I beg when there were more humans in the area than at a playoff hockey game, and I'm talking Canadian, not American. You folks really should support your teams more. Again, observations from my *wad*.

"Anything you need to say to me, you can say right here and now." She opened her purse, took out a miniature mirror, and checked her face.

I took a deep breath and plunged right in, just like the time I jumped off Mount Annable. "I need to go on your spaceship."

"You and about a gazillion other people who'd like to travel with me. Sorry, not going to happen." She snapped her purse closed and ended the conversation. "I already said no when Ralb asked, and if I said no to him, I'm certainly going to say no to you."

"But we go way back, we had some fun times in Bedrocktown." Okay, I couldn't think of anything off the top of my head, actually she had been a major pain in the butt since I landed. She picked on me, bullied me, and made my life a living heck, but she had to have some redeeming qualities that I could sum up. Okay, it was totally my fault I blamed her family for causing the *E. coli* outbreak in the town, but I was wrong and I admitted it. Reader, those adventures are more detailed in my first book, I was a Teenage ALIEN.

"Bedrocktown was so yesterday." She flicked her hair and grinned at the Entertainment Nighttime host.

"Oh, that's too bad. I was talking to him." I nodded in the direction of the ET commentator. "And he wants to do a whole half hour segment on your roots. We're organizing a parade, and they're naming a street after you." Okay, so it was all lies, but only little white ones.

A girl has to do what a girl has to do in the name of love.

"A street? I deserve more than a street." She huffed and puffed like she was the big bad wolf.

"See, that's what I told them too. I was thinking of a school or better yet, that new mall they're building on Hwy 7." I was rolling like a stone, gathering speed as I rolled. I was so going on the spaceship, Josh was going to become whole again, and we'd live happily ever after. "And the money raised from your mall appearance will go toward saving the penguins." There, I laid my final card on the table. If adding those little black-and-white birds to the mix didn't get Josh home, I'd be a monkey's aunt.

"Thanks for all your help in organizing it. When I get back from space, we'll fix a time." She leaned over and air kissed me. "We did have some good times, see you when I get back."

I deflated like a week-old helium balloon. Josh was a goner. But I couldn't, dang it, I wouldn't give up hope until the final second counted down.

There had to be another way.

Think, Oas, think.

Chapter 12

I was conscious of the time ticking away, edging ever closer to the period when Josh's life would be permanently irreversible. That was so not going to happen, not on my watch!

I telepathed my new plan to Rotsen, who of course had his own minor suggestions, which I took into account then completely ignored. Now I had to put it into effect with the wind in my hair and a song in my heart, even though my heart was still broken from my recent g-friendhood.

My minor celebrity brother, Nicola, and I walked along the red carpet and entered through the ten-foot-high double doors into the theater. I was expecting tables and some food—my stomach was rumbling like an erupting volcano—instead, there were seats, rows upon rows.

"We're with Suzzy," Ralb told the usher (not the singer, though I did see him across the room, and let me tell you if I wasn't in mourning…)

"Right, down to the front row, second from the end." He waved us along.

"Easy peasy." Ralb led us down the slight decline toward the stage, where crystal beads hung in a makeshift curtain, casting a cavalcade of colors.

"Yeah, except there are three of us, and they only counted on two people—you and your date." I let go of his elbow and scooted over so I could speak to Nicola.

"Hey, Nic, when we get to our seats, let's you and me hit the can." Remembering I wasn't in an episode of a sitcom, I rephrased. "I mean, will you accompany me to the washroom?"

"You betcha." She squeezed my arm. "I can't believe I found you again. I thought I'd never see you."

"Me too." Happiness seeped through my pores. Nicola and I had some great times together. She taught me so much about Earth, but more importantly she instructed me how to fit in as a teenage girl, something I will be eternally grateful.

"I'm sorry, Tollm. You're going to have to move back a row. Suzzy has an extra person," Beau Richardson's voice commanded. "I'm sure you don't mind, mate. Ralb here has two gorgeous women on his arm, and he shouldn't have to choose which one he gets to sit with."

Beau Richardson! Hotter than Zorca-twenty-three, and let me tell you, in the middle of a heat wave, our temps have been known to hit 350° Fahrenheit.

But more importantly, Suzzy's manager.

And did you notice? I sure did.

He called me gorgeous! Called *me* gorgeous!

His voice resonated as only a true gentleman's can. I'm sure you know what I mean. Sometimes a mawl speaks with such confidence, such self-assuredness one is forced to take him down a peg or three.

That person would be me.

Sometimes.

But now I had to coddle, schmooze, and generally make nice if I wanted a first-class seat on SpaceMoonOne. I had to grease some wheels, grease some palms, and grease anything else I could get my hands on.

Schmoozing is what I'd have to do.

And do well.

"Beau, is that you?" Ignoring the surprised looks of both Ralb (I don't know why he was surprised; he was well aware of my goal) and Nicola, I sidestepped between them and edged closer to Beau. I got into his space and inhaled the masculine scent that reminded me of a forest in the middle of a rainstorm.

Josh! Remember Josh! Maybe I could get to Suzzy through the back door if I sucked up to Beau.

"Yes, darling, how you all doing?" Beau asked with a smile.

See what I mean about a gentleman? He didn't have a clue who I was, had never met me in his life, and yet was too polite to mention it.

"I'm doing just fine, Beau." I took his arm and snuggled closer. "It's really my fault you're short a seat." I smiled up at him. I stood on my tippy-toes to whisper into his left ear, the one with the small, gold-hooped earring. "Let's not inconvenience Tollm and his guest. Ralb is my brother, and I would much rather sit beside you than him."

His Caribbean blue eyes gaze glided from my head to my toes, causing goose bumps to skittle across my skin.

I so wasn't impressed by him. He was the complete opposite from my Josh. Josh was down-to-earth, the type of guy who would take your heart and hold it forever. He would have put me on a pedestal and treated me like a queen. Beau might put me on a pedestal too, but only so he could look up my skirt.

I know the type. Total babe hound. And he knew how to use the dimple to his advantage, which he was, and it was definitely working.

Luckily, I was wise to his ways. I wasn't about to fall for his games, but—and it's a big but—I'd play his huge ego to my advantage. After all, he was no different than Gorget, different species, but a mawl all the same. Mawls were the same no matter what solar system. They wanted to feel wanted, needed, and above all adored. See, you don't need to read books (well just this one) on how to land a mawl, just follow those six words and you'll be fighting them off.

He checked his handheld device, which I'd seen last week in *Persone* magazine's 'What's Hot' section. It wasn't available yet, but Beau had one and, obviously familiar with it, typed without looking at the keys. Oh heavens, a total gadget head. He kept his eyes on mine as he typed.

"And where, darling, would you suggest we sit? Would you want to park yourself on my lap?" He slid his phone into his black tuxedo jacket and then grazed his knuckles against the back of my arm. He'd found a sensitive spot I didn't even realize I had. Wow.

Flustered, I took a step backward, right onto Ralb's foot.

"Hey, watch where you're stepping! You weigh a ton. All that pizza the other night went right to your hips."

"Ralb, how can you say this little lady is heavy? I bet I could throw her over my shoulder with one hand and take her away from here," Beau said with half-closed eyes, his gaze on my lips.

Oh heavens, he was winning the flirting game, and

it was so not going to happen. I had to get the upper mandible here, or I'd be hitchhiking on a passing asteroid or hanging on the outside of the rocket with Josh clinging on for dear death.

"Beau! Beau! *Beau!*" Suzzy's voice got higher in pitch the more he ignored her. This wouldn't help my cause with Josh, but I have to tell you it was very satisfying to have him completely ignore her.

"Beau, you're right. Why don't we blow this pop stand and go outside? I, for one, could use some fresh air." I leaned forward, knowing where his baby blue eyes were about to dip.

"Sure, babe." He turned around. "Suzzy, can you behave yourself for a couple of minutes while I take a bit of a breather?"

Suddenly she became deeply involved in a conversation with Stevey Spielhill, she waved her hand dismissively and turned her back to us.

"I'll be right back," I said to Nicola, who was too busy gaping at the stars to hear me.

I hooked my arm through Beau's and allowed him to lead us through an emergency exit and into an improvised smoking area. The air was filled with noxious gases, and blue clouds floated across the open-sided room, making me homesick for the nearby planet of Saturn.

"So, babe, where are you from?" Beau asked, as he fished in the pocket of his jacket. He withdrew a packet of cigarettes and tapped one into his palm.

I took a deep breath and accepted. I had to fit in with the cool guy. I had to step up to the plate and get on his good side. If it meant ruining my lungs for the rest of my life to save Josh's, I would do so.

He ran a hand through his hair, ruffling it up even more. "No worries. Hey, Mely, can I bum a light?" He leaned over, cupping his hand around the actor's cigarette, and then inhaled, blowing the smoke toward the sky. I really felt bad for the ozone layer. I've seen it up close and personal. With all the exhaust spewing out of your vehicles, it's no wonder the environment is in such bad shape.

I held the cigarette between my first two fingers, the way I'd seen it done in the movies I'd watched on my *wad* and leaned over as he nearly lit fire to my face.

I wasn't about to lecture him about the evils of smoking. I mean, I could tell him smoking turns your lungs from a pretty pink to black, black tar to be exact. I'm just saying it's not a pleasant thought. And to kiss someone who's been smoking is like licking an ashtray, and with my recent adventures in an ashtray, I didn't want to go anywhere near that again. Not that I was thinking of kissing him. I was a recent mawl-widow, and I wasn't about to go kissing the next mawl who asked.

"You know I never smoked until I took up with Suzzy. She is something else. I've managed some difficult peeps in my time, but she takes the cake." He paused and inhaled. "I know I could quit any time, but I need the crutch in my dealings with her."

Smoking can't be that hard to do. From what I understood, you were fine as long as you didn't inhale, at least according to some important people. I sucked my lips together, and breathed in.

Okay, don't think of smoke inhalation being bad for you. Ignore the fact that it feels like you're trapped in a burning house with the smoke billowing around and you can't breathe.

Think of Josh.

The smoke slithered into my lungs, swirling downward. I coughed.

I bent over, hacking. Lights flashed in front of my eyes as I tried to get some of Earth's unhealthy oxygen into my lungs.

I was about to die and all because I was trying to save Josh.

Suddenly Beau semi-gently slapped my back, and I righted myself. Spit dripped down my lip as I stood. I wiped it off with the back of my hand and straightened my backbone. I survived the wretched fumes racing through my body, touching each of my organs with an ugly vile stick, turning my new fresh organs an awful hue of black.

"I thought you knew how to smoke," Beau said, his hand still possessively on my back.

"Wouldn't it be better to find something that won't shorten your life?" I picked at a hangnail, trying to regain my composure. "You can't need a crutch that bad working with Suzzy. Why not try something which isn't going to kill you? Maybe like rock climbing or extreme hang gliding.

"Hey, babe. We all have to go sometime, and I want to enjoy what time I have here. If it means having a ciggy every once in a while, well, shoot me." Man, he was defensive.

"Shooting would be a quicker way to die than inhaling all those fumes." Wait a minute. I was supposed to be sucking up to him, not getting him on the offensive. Oas, shut up. You need to do better than this. What is it about this mawl? One minute I wanted to torture him more than Ralb, and the next I was concerned about his welfare.

"*Babe*, enough about my bad habits." He tucked a piece of my flyaway hair behind my ear. "Tell me about yours."

"My only bad habit is putting up with my brother." I smiled.

"He doesn't seem so bad," he said, puffing away like a dragon.

"That's because he has on his game face." I almost said Beau wouldn't want to see Ralb's real one—three big bug eyes and a set of antennas that could make your skin crawl. It amazed me that the same gene pool could, on one antenna, create someone as cute as Gorget and, on the other, also create someone as scaly and downright yucky as my brother.

"You avoided my question, babe. Where are you from?" He flicked ash from his cigarette. "I've never encountered an accent like yours before. Is it for real or a put on?"

Great! I hate it when I meet someone new, and they ask me that. Is it the most original thing an Earthling can come up with? Even better, "What's your sign?" Please! Get a life, read some books, and ask me a more thought-provoking question, like the origin of life. Now that's one I could answer, and let me tell you, you all didn't evolve from the seas. What a lame theory.

"I came from a place far away from here," I said, giving my stock answer. "Somewhere not nearly as green and lush as here."

"Let me guess—Canada."

Why is it that Ralb, and now Beau, think Canada is a cold, stark place where the Canadians all live in igloos and ride around in dog sleds? (Which I suspect is major fun!) Have they never read a book? Or watched a documentary on television? I can speak for my brother. If it isn't in a comic book, he isn't interested, but I'd hoped Beau was more educated.

"What have you got against Canada?" I asked, more curious than anything.

"Nah, nothing. My ex was from Toronto, and I really don't have much good to say about it." He inhaled the last of his cigarette and then threw it on the ground, allowing the butt to burn out. "But I don't want to talk about her. I'd much rather discuss you."

He searched his pocket and pulled out a package of gum. Happily, it didn't have Suzzy's face on the package but was rather a popular brand of strawberry-flavored gum. After offering me a stick, he unwrapped one and popped it in his mouth.

"Here, let me. A strand of hair is caught up in your earring." He leaned forward and ran a nicotine-stained finger through my hair.

"Umm, Beau, I have a favor to ask of you?" I reached over and flicked piece of dirt off his jacket.

"Ask away, babe."

I closed my eyes and thought of Josh, probably triggered by the smell of the gum—strawberry was his favorite. I pretended it was his fingers running through my hair, his fingers caressing my neck, his mouth breathing in my ear.

"I was wondering if you'd let me onto SpaceMoonOne." I kissed the tip of his nose and put my finger to his lips when he tried to kiss me. "It's just that my brother will always hang it over my head if he gets to go and I don't." When inventing a lie, keep as close to the truth as possible.

"Sure, babe," he murmured in my ear. "I have an older sister, she would totally be the same. She still rubs it in she got to go to Woodstock and I didn't, and I wasn't even born then."

"Really? I can go?" I squealed. "That's like totally awesome. I can't believe it. I get to go on SpaceMoonOne and see Zen."

"What do you mean, see Zen?" He leaned against the brick wall, arms crossed.

Shoot, once again my mouth wasn't connected to my brain, must be all the shape-changing that was toying with my noggin.

"Zen, I didn't say Zen, I said Ben. Look there's Ben over there." I shot my hand out and pointed to a gaggle of men standing by the far wall. "You probably just misunderstood me with my accent and all." Yes, brain is now connected to mouth. "Thanks again for letting me go with you all." Cripes, now I'd picked up Rotsen's fake Southern accent.

"No problem. I have an idea as to how you can thank me." He glanced over his shoulder toward the men, who circled in a football huddle, each with their back to us. Wasting no time, he pulled me closer and clamped his mouth on mine. His tongue darted into my mouth. Only the imagine of Josh's corpse kept me from biting down on it.

I was where thousands of femawls would give their *wads* to be, kissing Beau Richardson, but I felt like I was in a horror movie and about to open the door to the basement.

"Stop. I can't breathe." I tried to regain the upper hand, but he was forty pounds stronger. "Please, stop."

His mouth assaulted mine. A kiss should be a loving communication between two consenting adults. I wasn't agreeing to anything he was offering. A kiss should be the way it was between Josh and me. Like the first time Josh kissed me under the stars of Bedrocktown.

"Aww, Josh."

"Who the heck is Josh?" A voice jolted me out of my daydream. "Who the heck is Josh?"

Chapter 13

"Hey, get your hands off my sister." Ralb yanked Beau away from me and stood before us, his fists poised like a boxer waiting for a bout. Sure, now he wants to be my brother. He was turning on and off his loyalty like a kitchen faucet.

"Ralb, I'm okay." I rubbed the soreness from my wrists, too embarrassed to catch Beau's eye. Thanks to my big mouth, I'd be lucky if I ever got home unless I hung onto the side of the rocket. Vegas was always ready for a good gossip, so needless to say the entire smoking area had gone quiet. You could hear a cigarette butt drop as they all listened in.

"Really, Ralb, I'm fine," I repeated. "It was a slight misunderstanding, and I'm sorry."

"Nah, I'm the one who's sorry. I was a fool to think…never mind." Beau turned his back on me and headed toward the door but then stopped and faced Ralb. "Hey, bro, don't tease your sister too much about you being on SpaceMoonOne when she's stuck here on Earth." He turned and disappeared through the entrance without another backward glance.

"What was that all about?" Ralb asked through gritted teeth while nodding and smiling to the others in the smoking area.

"He caught me by surprise and kissed me. I wasn't ready for it." Major understatement. I would never willingly kiss anyone but Josh ever again. Ever is a long time, so I had to get onto SpaceMoonOne.

I had tried Ralb, Beau, and Suzzy, all without success.

"Can't you control yourself for one minute?" Ralb asked. "First of all, kissing him was so not part of the plan. And secondly, I will totally never—and I mean never—understand femawls. One minute you're *boo-hoo*ing over Josh, and the next you're locking lips with a complete stranger." He flung his hands in the air. "Femawls will be the death of me."

"Amen," a chorus of mawl voices rang out. I shot each of them a dirty look. Ralb should talk. He'd wasted his first Earth kiss on Suzz. Even before she became famous, she was the type of femawl who would talk sweet to your face while being four-faced, which is totally worse than two-faced times two. Totally not to be trusted, totally not to be tolerated, and totally not to turn your back on.

A bell rang, and the smoker's area emptied.

"I came to find you. The show's about to start, but I guess you've ruined all that." The vein in Ralb's neck popped out so far I could almost see the blood pulsing. "Figures, the one exciting moment in my life, and you've wrecked it."

Left-back-atcha, bro. "I'll make nice with Beau, and we'll be GtoG," I said with a self-assuredness I didn't feel. How could I face Beau and schmooze with him after this? But I had to get aboard the rocket one way or another. Obviously, he wasn't going to give up his seat, and I doubted it would be an option to sit on his lap all the way to the Space Port.

Looks like I might be hitchhiking through the

galaxy.

"Why didn't you just close your eyes, think of something pleasant while he was kissing you? Then there wouldn't be a problem," Ralb said. Rotsen, back in the land of the living, nodded his petals in agreement.

"You might like kissing people who turn your stomach, but not me."

"Yeah well, I'm the one heading to the Space Port. And you, dear little sis, are the one stuck here." He smirked.

"Ralb, I've got it." I pulled his arm to keep him from following the crowd back into the auditorium.

Ralb sighed. "I can't wait to hear this brainstorm. What great idea has the wise one come up with? Let me see now. You tried to suck up to Suzz, strike one. Then you tried to suck up to Beau, strike two. One more strike, and you're outta there."

Up until now, Rotsen had been quiet, no doubt lulled to sleep by the tobacco fumes. Dandelions don't do well in polluted environments. Plus, he would use any excuse to nap.

Yawning, Rotsen stretched his dandelion petals toward the sky and flexed his leaves.

"Let me guess, you're going to make a payoff to someone, or I know, I know—" Rotsen waved his petals like a kid in school who has to go to the bathroom. "You're going to whack someone. I know how to disguise your DNA so the cops never nab you."

"Neither, my dear crime show watching friend, I'm going to do something quite extraordinary, quite unbelievable, quite—"

"Would you get on with it?" Ralb said. "I'd still like to see some of the show before I'm eligible for an old age pension."

"We don't have time to see any of the show," I said. "Or at least I don't."

"Come on, what's the grand plan?"

"I'm going to sneak aboard and hide, like a stowaway. Wait here a sec." I ducked behind the planter and popped open my *hanaglug*. Grabbing my *mist book*, I flipped through the pages to find what I needed, carefully handling the pages where Josh's body was cemented.

"I'm back." I popped back around, tucking my *hanaglug* back into the tiny pocket.

Rotsen threw a leaf over his eyes. "This'll be a recipe for disaster."

I brushed my hands together as if cleaning off crumbs. "*Au contraire, mon ami*, it'll be a piece of double chocolate cheesecake."

Chapter 14

I had to get on SpaceMoonOne ASAP. There wasn't time to waste. I watched from the door of the auditorium as Ralb spoke to Nicola. Concern shadowed her face, and she left her prime seat to come over.

"Let's go," she said, placing her palm on my forehead.

"Come on, girlfriend, we're going to the bathroom."

With a stealthiness any spy would be proud of, she led me out the door and into a foyer where a drawing of a stick figure in a skirt indicated the women's washroom. What is it with those Vegas folks and their obsession with skinniness?

Once inside, Nicola checked all the stalls to make sure they were empty. A woman in a white starched dress was touching up her makeup with more wands and pots than any wizard ever dreamed of, but one look at Nicola's face, and she left the room.

"Okay, spill the beans, why the tears?" Nicola gently pushed me down onto one of the white sofas lining the walls.

Oh, this was going to be hard. Probably the hardest conversation I'd ever had. It was easier to breakup with Gorget. And it was easier to leave Earth the first time with Ralb at the controls even though who knew where we'd end up. She was sick, and I didn't want to burden her. But now if I made it onto SpaceMoonOne—and I would, whatever it took—I wouldn't be back to Earth in the near future, possibly wouldn't be back ever. And somehow, some way, I had to explain this to Nicola.

How do you tell your BFF you're an alien? And that I needed her help to change back into my true life form?

Chapter 15

"I think I know what you're going to tell me, and believe me, it's okay." Nic sat down beside me, placed her purse on the table, and wrapped an arm around my shoulders. "I kind of figured it out, so we're good."

"Really?" A megaton weight had been lifted off my shoulders. "I'm so glad you're okay with it." I sighed. "I really didn't know how I was going to break it to you that I'm an alien."

"Like your family is here illegally? That's okay, Suzz's father hired lots of people from other countries to run the farm." She picked up a tissue and began to fold it into a flower shape.

"Not that kind of alien, more in line with Area fifty-one alien." I hated to lump myself with those Edoricks, they are what you humans consider aliens, as they are the stupidest aliens in the solar system. I mean, they are so dumb you humans know about them.

"Alien!" She threw the tissue at me, jumped off the sofa, and headed across the room and sat on the other sofa, drawing her knees up in protection.

"Geez, Nicola, it's not like I'm a mouse or a spider." I glanced in the mirror across from me and saw my neck was red, the color creeping up my face. I mean, it's not like a person can help where they come from. I mean, if people could, would anyone really want to live in famine-stricken countries? And it's not like I had a say when my parents decided to settle on a planet not in your galaxy.

"Nic, I'm not about to do anything to harm you, I love you. You're my BFF, and I don't use that title easily." I mean, I did save her live, not that that should really account for anything.

"Yeah, remember when you and Suzz first met me, in the forest by the lake?" When she nodded, I said, "I had just landed via an asteroid."

"Really? You looked really good." She picked at the nail polish on one of her manicured fingernails. "You looked like you'd just stepped off a runway."

"Umm, thanks." Of course, that had me bursting with pride. I mean, how many people can travel through space, dodging meteorites and maneuvering through black holes and be complimented on how hot they look when they arrive? Especially since I'd been channeling Peddy Bundt from *Living with My Children* reruns at the time. Is it any wonder Nic is my BFF?

"Go on." She creased her brow, not a good habit to get into unless she wanted to visit the Botox doctor in the not-too-distant future, and settled back on her couch, apparently ready to hear the rest. "So, you're from another galaxy?" Nicola asked, now more curious than scared. "What's your planet like? Are there malls?" This is the Nicola I know and loved.

"Not too far away, near the Space Port. And the only mall we have is the Black Hole. My planet basically looks like Vegas on a bad day without the neon and glitz, just rocks and plants." I paused. "Kinda boring, actually. That's why I couldn't wait to come here and meet earth people. You sure didn't disappoint."

"Black Hole, isn't that where you got that cool outfit you had on when you landed?"

I nodded, and she continued. "Wow, you have really cool shops. So, did you study me? Am I going to be written up in books?" She sat up straighter.

"No, I studied how you walked and talked so I could fit in. Well, fit in as much as an alien teenager could."

"Is Ralb an alien too? Did he do a mind test on me to get me to break up with Owen and out with him? She turned a light shade of green. I wasn't sure if it was because she kissed an alien or realized she kissed my brother, either would make me feel barfy.

"We don't do mind tricks, you have to blame yourself for liking my brother, and yes, he's an alien too, but I need your help." I came out with it.

"I thought all alien life forms were superior to ours. Can't you like travel at the speed of sound or light or something? Do you have a cool UFO? Where is it?" She glanced into the bathroom stall, like I crash landed it there. "Is it in Area fifty-one?"

"I came down via an asteroid." Jeez, I loved her, but she had to start paying attention. Changing the subject, I continued. "I need your help."

"You saved my life. You were the only one who caught on to the fact I was a victim of *E. coli* poisoning, this is the least I can do. What do you need help with? I'm not going to kill anybody for you." She kept her distance across the room.

"Josh is dead, and I need to get him home." Shoot, maybe I shouldn't have led with that.

"Did you kill him?" Nicola bolted for the door and had one hand on the handle.

"Of course not, I loved, er, love him. Suzz stepped on him and smacked him. But my planet can revive him if I can get him there soon enough." I paused, suddenly exhausted by the day's events. I was facing major travel lag.

"Figures. How can I help?" She sank down in the chair beside me but kept her body tight and away from mine.

"I have to get Josh home, but I ruined my chances to get on SpaceMoonOne in my Earth form." I paused, trying to think best how to word it. "I need to morph back into my alien form."

"How do you do that?" Nicola squished together her eyebrows. "Do I abra-kadapter you? Or do you howl at the full moon?"

"I'm an alien, Nic, not a werewolf. Really though it's not that difficult. I just need salt."

"Salt? Like normal table salt?" She shook her head. "I'm really kind of disappointed."

"Gee, I'm sorry it's not something more exciting, but really I need your help and even more so, Josh needs your help." I was kind of ticked off. Time was a wasting, and she was upset because I didn't have a more elaborate method of shape changing.

"Come on, I know where we'll find salt." She grabbed my hand, picked up her purse from the table and pulled me out of the chair. "You saved my life; I'll save yours and Josh's. I should be in line for some good karma for this one."

Chapter 16

We rubbed shoulders, and in one case knees, don't ask, but let's just say when the tabloids say a certain actor drinks himself under the table, he in fact does. Nic was like the bull in the running of the bulls. She had a one-track mind, and nothing and no one was going to get in her way.

She nodded to Leep, waved to JayKK, and fist pumped Katgy. She paved our way clear to the buffet table. In keeping with the theme of the night, the table was shaped like a giant interlocking TZZ. The table groaned under the weight of the food. Sliced kiwis lay in mile long rows alongside chopped pineapples. Oranges, limes, and lemons cut in quarters, each sitting together as a whole. A chocolate fountain gurgled beside a cupcake tree which reached to the ceiling, untouched.

Nicola surveyed the food and sighed. "There's nothing with salt. Won't something else work?" She paused. "What about kumquats?"

"No, it has to be salt." I moaned. Stupid Zorca-twenty-three. Why couldn't it be something readily acceptable in fat-conscious Vegas?

"I've got an idea." Nicola pulled me out past the buffet and into the casino. The room was crowded with award show patrons, machines ringing, the walls covered with ads for restaurants and nightclub shows.

She whipped a dollar bill out of her purse and slid it into the slot machine. "Keep your fingers crossed."

I did and everything else that was crossable.

It must have worked because coins rained down into the little slots like we'd won the lottery, which I guess we did.

"Now you're going to lick them." Nic ordered, scooping them up into a little cup. "You'll get the salt off the people's fingers that's on the coins.

Major grossness, but I knew I had to do it for Josh. For Josh I would do anything, even suck on dirty coins.

As I put the first coin in my mouth, Nic whipped my hand away, the coin flying across the room and almost hitting an elderly patron in the face. He grinned toward us and raised his glass.

"I've got a better idea." Nic grabbed my arm, pointed at the sign, and pulled me out of the casino. At this rate, one of my arms was definitely going to be longer than the other, not a pretty sight.

"Where are we headed? I can't be gone too long. I have to get on the spaceship." I groaned.

"And you will. Here we are." She stopped in front of Salt Lake BBQ and caught her breath. "If they don't have salt, no one will."

Ignoring the small booth and the startled waitress, Nic smiled but bypassed her and headed straight for the kitchen.

"Why not take the salt off the table?" I whispered as we walked by an unoccupied table. "They're right there."

"I've got a better idea," Nicola bragged.

Great, surely it had to be better than licking coins.

"You can't go in there," the miffed waitress

reprimanded us.

"Yes, we can. It's an emergency." Nic bulldozed her way past and entered the swinging doors, ducking to avoid a waiter carrying a tray of pulled pork. "My friend here is having a medical emergency and needs salt."

A bemused overweight cook, his chef's hat tilted to the left, wordlessly handed Nic a box of salt before turning back to the pig hanging over a spit.

"Thank you. Come on, let's go. You've got a spaceship to catch."

With the speed of a distance runner, we headed back to the event and back to the familiar scene of the bathroom. Luckily it was empty, and Nic moved the chair behind the door, blocking anyone else entering.

"Ok, show me what you do." Nic sat down in the chair. "This is really kind of cool."

"Nic, I really don't know how to thank you. You are amazing, the best BFF ever." My eyes welled up as if they were filled with salt, and I put the plug in the sink and turned on the taps. "You are way too good for my brother. He doesn't deserve you."

I added the salt to the water and leaned over the sink, sucking it up like one of those anteaters on your nature shows, again something I learned from my *wad*.

My body shook, my eyes rolled back into my head, and my three eyes sprung out in their place. Hair was replaced, skin with scales. I glanced into the mirror and saw Nic's reaction. Her mouth was gaping, her eyes bulging, but other than that she appeared to be accepting of my morphis.

A knock interrupted the silence and Ralb's frantic voice came through the door. "Oas, we have to get going *now*!"

In semi shock Nic pulled the chair away from the door and Ralb fell forward into the room.

"Hi, Nicola." His eyebrows rose in shock as he looked around the room like an owl, his head swiveling 360 degrees, his hands full of glam giveaway gift bags. "Oas, really we have to go."

"Have all the celebrities seen what a fake you are?"

"Beau is out for your head, and we have to get you on SpaceMoonOne without him realizing you're on board."

"Shouldn't be too hard now." I sat on the side of the sink, my head bobbing between his face and Nic's. "Come on, we've got to get Josh home."

"Right, it's all about Josh." Ralb shrugged his shoulders. "Nic, this isn't goodbye."

Oh God, here we go. Lovely dovey goodbyes make me want to gag, especially when I wasn't involved.

"Nic, we can keep in touch via satellite, so it's really not goodbye. I'll e-mail you when I get back to Zorca-twenty-three, and we can chat on Rockface." I hurried them along by reminding them I was in the room.

"The Internet can communicate to other planets?" she asked, her eyes wide, blinking uncontrollably. "Will you promise to e-mail me?"

I nodded, but she was looking at Ralb, not at me. I would so have to e-mail her and tell her all his bad points. I hope my hard drive is big enough.

Chapter 17

Clouds played peek-a-boo with the moon as we left the auditorium. Away from the bright strobe-lit red carpet, the darkened side streets were relatively quiet after the hubbub of the event. I breathed deeply, inhaling clean air void of cloying perfumes and strong aftershave. My semi oxygen-deprived lungs sucked it up probably afraid I'd subject them to more nicotine.

Block after block we went, the lights from the TZZ event eventually fading to a distant gray.

"So Nic handled our news quite well." I poked my head out of the Mgg gift bag, my mandibles gripping onto the side. Rotsen had conveniently wrapped himself around the gold cord handle, and Josh was safely tucked in the bottom inside my *mist book* beside a very expensive watch, which I was totally giving him. After the grief Ralb put me through it was the least he could do for us.

"Yeah, well, next time try and keep your trap shut and don't tell my girl I'm an alien, kind of a mood killer if you know what I mean." Ralb flicked the bag hard, and I almost flew out the top.

"Oh no," Rotsen said. "I really wouldn't go there if I were you, Ralb. Man, how naïve you are in dealing with femawls."

"What? She did kill the mood," he grumbled.

"Her mawlfriend is dead; I think she has more

important things on her mind than worrying about butchering the mood with your femawlfriend," Rotsen explained simply.

"How did you get to be so smart?" Ralb asked, flinging the bag with even more intensity.

"I take notes. Listen to femawls and you can't go too far wrong." Rotsen shrugged his leaves. "It's not rocket science."

"How many more miles till we get there?" I whined. We had passed more brand name stores than I've ever seen in a mall. Figures when I wasn't in the shape or mood for shopping, that's when we hit all the shopping centers. Major conspiracy. I'd already counted three coffee shops, and if I wasn't held hostage in this bag, I would have stopped for an extra-large strong brew. We are so going to have to get a coffee house on Zorca-twenty-three. Why hadn't they brought up that secret recipe like the astronauts did for burgers in paper wrappers and soda which had been a big hit with the young ones on our planet, especially since we could burp out our antennas? The adults of course, not so much. My Parental Being had to apologize sooo many times to the other Parental Beings as I was the one who found it on the Space Port.

"Can we stop for a coffee?" I whined more than once, but my requests fell on deaf ears. "Come on please, this shape shifting has really zoned me out, and I definitely need the caffeine."

"No way, you will get addicted and I am so not facing our Parental Beings when you start to go through withdrawal."

I stuck my forked tongue out at Ralb. Why of all my other roughly six hundred siblings did I have to end up with him here?

We went from the posh stores into a Chinese neighborhood. I held my breath as we passed a store with animal carcasses hanging on silver hooks, their bodies swinging slightly as we rushed by. As a vegetarian, (hey, remember, my true form is a praying mantis) I could so not see the point of eating meat. I know Lehcarr, my Venus flytrap BFF, loves meat, but only as a last resort. I try to live by the philosophy to not eat anything with a face. Of course, I had to sample the burgers in paper wrappers when I ventured onto the Space Port, but other than that, I've pretty much stuck to my ideal.

Where was Lehcarr? She was with us in France, and while Rotsen is here where was my BFF?

"Hey, anyone know where Lehcarr is?" I asked panic stricken.

"Calm down, she's with our Parental Beings. She wanted to head back to Zorca-twenty-three with them, and you'd know this if you weren't so busy making google eyes at Josh." Ralb explained.

"You don't have to sound so condescending."

Like a two-faced dandelion, Rotsen sided with Ralb and flung words back at me. "Ralb is doing all the work, let's have some patience with him and *moi* for everything I've had to put up with."

I just loved how neither one of them was giving me a break after what I'd gone through today. How come there's no, "Sorry for your loss, Oas" or even a measly pat on the back of my wings to comfort me, much less sharing my grief? Negatory! Zippo!

"Oh please. Tell me, oh wise one, what on Earth— or Zorca-twenty-three—you're going on about?" I stopped short, both to catch my breath and to haul Ralb to a stop so I could be face to face with Rotsen.

Rotsen pointed a leaf at me like he was suddenly the teacher and me the disobedient student. "Listen, it wasn't my choice to come here. I had to come, forced beyond my control. Zen sent me to ensure you didn't screw things up here too much." He paused, now he seemed to be gathering steam, and not in a good way. "I am a highly trained individual who's been reduced to a full-time babysitter."

"No one asked you to come." I snorted. "Well, Zen did, but he doesn't count. You know what a pushover he is. You could have just said no and stayed home."

"I owed him. I had to come, and you don't know how much I want to go home." He ruffled his petals. "I'm counting the hours until we're all on SpaceMoonOne and heading back to Zorca-twenty-three."

"You and me both." Ralb sighed. He wiped sweat from his brow and unbuttoned his suit jacket, then he kicked off his shoes and rubbed his feet. Yuck, nothing is uglier than your brother's bare feet, but I guess they were sore from the miles he walked.

"If I remember the situation correctly, it was because of Ralb we both had to venture to this stupid planet. So, don't yell at me that I was the one who needed babysitting." I raised my voice several octaves. "He was the one who wouldn't answer his nose piece and come home. He was the one who screwed up the mission by falling for an Earth girl and refusing to come back to Zorca-twenty-three." I folded my mandibles and pouted. Needless to say, I was some pissed *out*.

In the distance, I could see a large spotlight on SpaceMoonOne, the Vegas sign in the background. Apparently, we were launching from the back of the TZZ studio lot. Who needs an official launch site!

"Let's get a move on," I called back over my shoulder. "It's right in front of us." From somewhere in the depths of my soul, I found a renewed source of energy that propelled me onward. Like I was following the North Star, I directed Ralb toward the monstrosity in front of us, never taking my eyes off it, as if afraid it would disappear.

SpaceMoonOne stood like a beacon in the middle of the launch pad, dwarfing the apartments and office buildings of the studio around it. It reminded me of a giant firecracker, and I clung tightly onto the bag to stare at it.

The rocket was beautiful—smooth and white, glowing, tall and proud against the sky for the entire world to see. The American flag decorated the side, along with logos from three major sporting goods companies and the Sn logo prominently displayed. After so much negative publicity with athletes, the companies have now decided to launch their trademarks into space. I wasn't sure if they planned on recruiting alien life forms to their brands, or what, but it seemed tacky.

Although the rocket towered over us, Ralb still had to walk six miles to get to the secured area—and he wasn't a fan of climbing over barbed-wire fences, probably afraid of tearing his pants. The wire surrounding the field prison-like seemed a little extreme. It wasn't like the rocket was going to escape or anything. And really, who in their right mind would venture inside and try to hitch a ride? I mean, geez, we had to be the only ones.

"Okay, Rotsen, since you were previously a secret agent, a super spy, so to speak, tell us how we're going to circumvent the fence and get inside the restricted area?" I asked, as we all ducked to avoid the strobe light which was sweeping by and highlighting the perimeter of the field. Signs plastered on the fence every ten feet warned *Trespassers Will Be Shot*. Not a favorable sign by any stretch of the imagination.

"Sure, now when the poop is about to hit the fan, you ask me for help," Rotsen said. "I seem to remember being stuck in a bedroom in Nicola's house while you two were partying it up, eating pizza and drinking soda till all hours of the night."

I glanced over at Ralb, who rolled his eyes Zorcanward. "Okay, we're sorry. We are young and stupid. We know what we did was wrong, and we promise we'll make it up to you as soon as we can as soon as we get home." He spread his hands. "When we get back, we'll treat you to anything you'd like. I know, we'll take you out to dinner, and we'll pay." He grabbed my mandible and held on tight, no doubt hoping I'd focus on the pain, not on his words.

"Fine, it's not like I haven't heard it all before, but whatev," Rotsen said, dropping his New York Mafia accent and speaking like an upper crust Brit. Maybe it was the attitude, but I wasn't about to fall for it. "So, my peeps, it's really elementary how we're going to get inside the compound."

Ralb tossed the bag onto a semi flat rock, and it was only due to my balancing skills I kept from sliding off the rock. Glancing around, I saw in my immediate eyesight shrubs and brush abound. Sounds of the night filled my ears. The area was filled with creepy crawly things in the middle of the night, and even though on my planet I might have been one of those creatures, I wasn't about to take a leap in the dark where I didn't know. Rotsen put out both leaves like he was surfing at Big Sur.

"Start walking, Ralb!" Rotsen ordered.

I jumped up, the bag slipping farther down the rock. "Are you kidding me? We're just going to walk in the front door." I stopped, surprised at the simplicity. "Righto. Ralb is an invited guest, and he can just sneak us on board."

"Well, I thought of it first," Rotsen bragged.

Like a parade of one, I scrambled into Ralb's hand, and he walked around the perimeter of the fence to the check point.

"Hello, anyone forgetting anything?" Rotsen called out, still attached to the bag's handles.

"Wait, you forgot Josh and Rotsen." I pinched his hand to get his attention. "Go back and get it. Josh is in there."

"Geez Louise, can't you do a simple thing like keep track of your dead mawlfriend?" Without further comment Ralb turned back to the rock and snarkily grabbed the bag. "Would you kindly hang onto him?" With great purpose he strutted back toward the fence.

"Halt!" A guard with a cheap imitation of a layered Jayt Bee haircut, his shoulders slouched like a wannabe hunchback, spaghetti sauce dripping down his chin, a C-grade actor in a B-movie, he bellowed "Who goes there?"

Apparently, since the rocket was a publicity stunt

for TZZ they'd decided to staff it themselves. No doubt he wasn't a real guard and the gun on his hip was probably a water pistol. He was probably the only actor within a fifty-mile radius who wasn't at the auditorium we'd just left. Easy peasy to get inside, and we'd be on our way home to where I can rightly reinstate Josh.

I glanced over toward Ralb to confirm he still had the bag that contained my first true love. Yes, *first* true love, and that includes Gorget from my home planet. I don't count someone who took my pulsating heart, broke it, and then stomped on it before canoodling with the Zorca-twenty-three equivalent of Suzz. A total slutkis!

"Right! Ralb, I see your name on the list." The guard, whose name badge read Alvin, tucked his clipboard under his arm and held out his hand to Ralb.

"It's a real honor to meet you, sir," Alvin said. "I've always wanted to shake hands with someone who won a contest. I figure it might bring me luck as well."

A braying sound interrupted him, getting louder in volume. We turned our heads as one and took in the animated display. Five Rockhopper penguins, their extra-long head feathers reminded me of a fascinator I saw at the recent British royal wedding which I got up at 2 am to watch on my *wad*.

"I don't know whose great idea it was to have automated Rockhopper penguins beside the spaceship, but I'd like to kick him in the butt," Alvin complained, pointing at the display. "Then I have to load these pains in the butts onto the ship and ensure the temperature in the cargo area is a mild thirty-eight degrees Fahrenheit so they can go into a comatose state to save their batteries."

Ralb turned his head and laughed. "Do you mean to tell me those little fellows aren't real?" He bent over to touch one and was promptly bitten on the hand. "Ouch, what the heck?"

"They aren't real, but a really good fake. I mean, they are used for movies." He leaned over to whisper to Ralb mawl to mawl. "They are part of the plan. That's all I can tell you."

Wow, there were more subplots here than in an episode of the Samsons. Again, the *wad*. Really you should invest in one.

Ralb leaned forward and squinted at the name tag. "Well, Alvin, it's a real pleasure to meet you, and I love the haircut." Oh my gosh, what was my brother doing? Schmoozing with a guard-slash-actor?

"Really! Do you like it? It's a copy of the one that hot pop star is wearing, you know where you just wash it and shake your head like a dog and it all just lies in place." Alvin grinned. "My gal did a great job cutting it."

"It looks great," Ralb said, keeping one eye on the largest of the penguins, which kept hopping over the rock nearest to him.

"Yeah, I have my autograph book all ready." He pulled a small book from an inside pocket of his uniform jacket and propped it open. "I've got one here from Jean Connolly, Peter Smithword, John Lennongrad, and the one I'm proud of the most so far, is Andy Jackson."

I consider myself a young and hip femawl, well-versed in the ways of Earth, but to be honest, I haven't heard of any of those folks.

"So, once I get Suzzy's I'll be able to sell it and

make a fortune." He grinned again, displaying chipped and stained teeth. I hoped he'd use the money for deodorant and maybe two new front teeth. I'd only been near Alvin for a few minutes, but I'd already sidled to Ralb's shirt cuff farthest away to stand downwind.

With a swish and a sway, Suzzy strolled up the catwalk like she was on a runway. Camera flashbulbs flashed like synchronized Christmas tree lights. I have to admit the little farm girl from Bedrocktown was a sight to see. She'd really branded herself, and I grudgingly admitted to myself that she was a pro, but then again she'd had a lot of practice. Even in her small hometown, she was a force to be reckoned with. I remember after I'd landed on Earth and was getting my bearings, (and, yes, cursing Ralb once again as a stone from the rocky beach bruised me, wondering why he couldn't have picked Barbados to visit, where the beaches are soft and romantic) when I first met Nic and Suzz. My first impression, and this will show you what a great judge of character I am, I said to myself, "Self, keep your friends close and your enemies closer." So, I stuck like glue to Suzz. Even back then, she was a big fish, the big shark in the little pond called Bedrocktown.

Vegas didn't stand a chance.

She flashed her teeth, which I knew for a fact were capped and painted more than the Sistine chapel. Her custom-made spacesuit was unzipped to her navel, her pants tighter than any jeans I'd ever seen. The advertisements across her shoulders and torso brought prominent attention to those areas a girl wants mawls' eyes to go.

"You go right ahead through, sir. There's a guard

farther in who will get you suited and seated up for your space adventure." Alvin bent down and waved Ralb through like he was royalty. Great! Now there would definitely be no living with him. His ego would be so big it could propel us to Zorca-twenty-three without any jet fuel. "One thing, though, sir." He pointed to the Mgg bag and whispered, his back turned to Suzzy. "We can't allow that bag on the ship."

I swallowed and glanced up at Ralb.

"Mgg didn't pay a royalty to advertise on the ship. I have strict instructions that no logos that aren't endorsed by Suzzy are allowed. Cameras are going to be filming, and we can't show an Mgg logo when she's paid by Carter." Alvin puffed up with authority.

"No worries, man. I'll just tuck it here in the bush and get it when I come back."

The guard shook his head negatively. "No can do. We can't have that product on the set."

"What is that bag doing near my ship?" Suzzy asked her entourage filling up the rest of the bridge. Addressing Alvin, she continued, "Didn't we say no Mgg? What are you, stupid?"

She took the bag by the cord handle and pitched it like she was in a caber toss.

Silently we watched the bag spin and carrel through the night air, the neon Mgg logo spiraling in the lights.

With Josh inside.

Chapter 18

"That wasn't a good idea." Ralb grimaced as he rubbed his left wrist, where I'd taken up temporary residence, my pinchers pinching him like there was no tomorrow, which as far as I was concerned there wasn't. He had to retrieve Josh.

Ignoring him, Suzzy played to the cameras which were now crowded around. "Let that be a lesson to all who didn't want to sponsor my spaceship flight. I will not tolerate your logos anywhere near *my* cameras." She licked her lips like the cat that ate the rest of the cream. "Now should we venture onto my ship, and I'll show you around. Come along, Ralb."

"What can I do?" He telepathed to me and Rotsen.

"How about growing a pair?" Rotsen voiced what I thought.

"Just a sec, Suzzy, I need to tie my shoe." With that he bent down, his mouth mere millimeters from me. "Go and get Josh, I'll wait for you here." He flicked me off his wrist before standing up. Rotsen wrapped his body around mine, and I now wore a dandelion hat as we raced off.

****

"That's a good one, Suzzy, er, Ms. Newsworthy," Alvin said. "Would you mind signing my autograph book?" With the speed of a jaguar, he whipped out the small rectangular book with a picture of Suzzy on the cover and handed her a pen.

"Turn around, Ralb, I need to use your back." Without waiting for an answer, she spun him around and forced him to bend over. "Sorry, chum, this pen doesn't work very well. Do you have another one?"

I stopped, but honestly, I couldn't stand still while she played drama-queen-slash-actress. I didn't stay to watch the performance, I had to find Josh.

Brush, dirt, and debris lay in front of me as I ducked and dodged around them. Cripes, why couldn't it be a direct line to where my Josh lay? Instead, I had to skitter across a maze, left, then right, then back to the left. At one point, I bumped into a large rock, my head ringing from the force. I had to slow down. I had to stay calm. I scurried into one bag, only to walk out backward, an annoyed rat facing me down.

"Sorry, sorry." I stood on my back legs, my front mandibles in my familiar praying stance. "Wrong bag."

Without turning my back on the vermin, I continued. The slight desert breeze wasn't making the tracking of my Josh any easier. What was I going to do if the ship took off before I could locate him? What if I failed?

Negative nilly thoughts weren't allowed.

Come on, Oas, you can do it.

Tired, exhausted, defeated, I sat down on a small bush, the coarse needles jabbing at my back. I sighed and looked around. The beacon-like spaceship was front and foremost in my line of sight, the brightest glowing off the Mgg neon logo.

What?

It was right in front of me. With a renewed energy that appeared out of nowhere, almost like I'd drank a king-sized version of those energy drinks, I ran-skipped to the bag and ducked inside. There was my *mist book,* appearing almost like a mirage. I felt in the pocket for my Josh and cautiously unwrapped the tissue. Tears dripped onto his carcass as I surveyed the shape and condition of my poor mawlfriend.

His leg was wrapped around his head in a unique yoga position, and one antenna was squished against his torso. I used my little finger and shifted his body to see if I could find the other antenna, the one which as a praying mantis we use to show our affections by hooking it together with our true love's.

"Okay, my little mawl. We're going to make your dream come true. Somehow we're going to get on that frigging spaceship and I'm going to show you my planet." I gently stroked his body as I whispered to him.

"Oas!" Rotsen pointed over toward the rocket. Clouds of gas and fumes hid the bottom portion. "I think they're revving up."

With delicate hands, I rewrapped Josh and tucked him into my *hanaglug.* It's an item you folks on Earth should really consider using. It shifts in size from a small backpack to a medium-sized suitcase, to a piece of chalk, depending on what's inside. Right now, it only contains my souvenirs from my travels and my poor Josh. Easy as a fold-up umbrella, it slid into an even smaller shape so I was able to fit it in the palm of my hand.

Without a backward glance, I grabbed it and ran toward the spaceship like there were a thousand zombies after us.

A floodlight illuminated the first gate, and as I approached the stone wall, I hid alongside and Rotsen flicked his dandelion head around the corner.

"Alvin and his chipped mug have left the scene," Rotsen said in a hushed tone. "Hmm."

"What do you see?"

"Nothing, nothing, other than that he's got his computer up and there appears to be video from a camera inside Suzzy's house."

"Would you quit watching television? We've got a rocket ship to catch! Rotsen, we so don't have time for this!"

"Right, sorry," Rotsen said, continuing to peer around the corner.

"Where is Ralb? He promised to wait for us." My small alien chest deflated.

"Really, are you surprised?" Rotsen telepathed, as my sibling's familiar laugh resonated through the ship.

"I don't really think it can be good for us inhaling those gases," Rotsen complained, using his petals to cover his face so only his eyes poked out. "Can't you walk a little faster?"

"I'm going as fast as I can. Would you like to get down and walk?" Geez, it was like talking to a child sometimes with him. Here he was moaning because he'd had to come and "rescue us", and all he did was complain. Well, when I got back to Zorca-twenty-three, I was so going to be rid of him and Ralb. They were no longer going to be a part of my life, and I didn't care.

I skittered up to the door of the spaceship, the metal slowly clanging shut. The stupid door didn't go to the bottom, creating a short step, a step which would be no more than a foot high if I was a humanoid, but since I was in my Zorca-twenty-three form, it was a Mount Annable I was facing.

"Come on, Oas, jump," Rotsen urged. "The door is about to shut. We've got to get on board."

"I c-c-c-can't. It's useless, Rotsen. I can't." I tried to climb up the smooth exterior of the ship, only to slide back down like I was on a vertical ice-skating rink. "We can't do it."

"Can't is not in your vocabulary." Rotsen smacked me across my antenna with his petals. "Why do you think you have *wings*?"

"Right, I forgot. I never use them on Earth, and I completely forgot I had them. You know I once received an award on Zorca-twenty-three for holding my wings in a straight line the longest." I paused in my ramblings to kiss Rotsen on his petally head. "You are a wise dandelion."

The door began to close as dry ice steamed out from the bottom of the ship.

"Oas!" His tone had more warnings than a poison label. "The door is shutting."

"OMG, you're right. Hang on, Rotsen." I untucked my wings from their prone position. I shook my back, and the stiffness and crampiness of the unexpected actions caused my stomach to flutter. Putting the discomfort behind me, I flapped my wings, and we were airborne. With the dry ice, the commotion of the Rockhopper penguins whose animation appeared to be short circuiting, and the heat from the engines, I almost misjudged the door opening.

The door slammed shut, and we were safely inside, well almost. We fell down onto the floor and as I tried to move and found I couldn't.

One of my stupid, barely used wings was caught in the door.

I couldn't move without tearing off my wing.

Tears flooded through my three eyes, and I sank down on the floor in my familiar praying mantis yoga pose.

"Rotsen, why is it nothing ever goes my way? I'm just one big screw up. I'm totally useless."

Rotsen wrapped his leaves around me and put his face toward mine. "Look at me right now," he ordered, and since I didn't have any choice, I did, before he continued, "You got us on the ship, you, not your brother, but you. You did it without anyone's help but your own."

"You told me to use my wings." I wiped my eyes and dripping nose with my mandible.

He grinned. "Well, that's true, but you did it. You got us on board for Josh. If that's not the most unselfish act I ever heard then I don't know what is."

"I guess so." I sniffed.

"So quit with the waterworks, and let's get this party started."

The room we'd entered looked like your typical garage on Earth. It seemed to be filled with the kind of junk nobody wants to look at but still needs to keep. Row upon row of terrariums, aquariums, and metal cages filled with an odd assortment of monkeys, dogs, pigs, and even a llama whose neck was bent in the small wire confinement. The creature's soulful eyes caught mine, and he flicked long eyelashes in sorrow.

Food supplies were packed alongside the cages—pyramid-style stacks of soup cans, dehydrated microwavable food packages, and bottles of water. Boxes of her flavored gum were stacked six high and five deep.

"I see pizza." I jumped up—I never could resist the thought of eating pizza. Forgetting my wing was caught in the door, a corner of it ripped off like yesterday's bandage.

I walked over for a closer look and saw the traveling reality show participants would not be without pizza, chips, or chocolate chip cookies and stifled a laugh over the gluten-free oatmeal cookies. This show was going to be real cutting edge. My stomach growled at the thought of the pizza—gooey cheese dripping down a triangle of rich yummy dough. I couldn't help myself. I reached over into the box and swiped a piece. I noted the logo on the box was one of the logos covering Suzzy's left breast. Don't know the significance of that, but I'm sure there was one.

"Did it hurt?" Rotsen asked, eyeing the web-like wing still in the door.

"Nah, I'm a femawl. Enough said."

Chapter 19

The pizza tasted wooden, like a chewable piece of cardboard, but then I'd never been a fan of that particular company's brand of food. (Yes, I know, I'm criticizing one of the staples of your planet.) Surely, they'd packed enough so one little piece wouldn't be missed. It would be just horrible if say, for example, Suzzy had hunger pains in space. Wouldn't that be the kicker on the reality show? Or even worse if Ralb happened to be the one left without food? Major horrors.

What is it with pizza? I sneaked another piece and ignored the dirty look and annoying cough from Rotsen.

"Fine," I said, giving Rotsen the crust. "I don't find it that great anyway, but beggars can't be choosers I guess."

He flashed me another dirty look and murmured with a full mouth, "It really needs soda to wash it down."

"Well, too bad we don't have time for a pizza party," I reminded him.

A metal spiral staircase led upward. I sprinted up the stairs like a bug on steroids before he could change his mind. If Rotsen had his way, we'd be eating pizza all night long. Apparently, the cheese and garlic don't affect dandelions, he didn't seem to gain an ounce.

Around and around I went up the twisted steps, passing a level that had more dials and control buttons than an airplane. The room was self-contained with one door, three chairs bolted in the middle, and a small trap door, with an unlit Exit sign above it. The buttons flashed red, white, and yellow, making sounds like a teakettle just before it whistles. I resisted the urge to touch the control panels—everything was so white, so smooth, and so new. The strong smell of plastic combined with a smattering of metal tickled my nose, but before I could sneeze I continued up to the next level. I squeezed through a door, wishing I hadn't had the extra piece of pizza, but I stopped so suddenly I almost fell back down the stairs.

Standing in the corner of the room in front of a slightly open cupboard door was a sight that made my blood run cold.

Major yuckness!

Ralb and Suzzy were in a lip lock!

Chapter 20

I stood dead still, watching my brother necking with the teen heartthrob. His eyes were closed, his head tilted to the left, but Suzzy looked like she was searching for the right camera angles. I followed her gaze to a black semi-circular globe on the ceiling. I knew from the department store when Nic took me clothes shopping in Bedrocktown it was a camera. At this rate, my bro was going to be on *Open H-wood* before we'd even lifted off. Suzzy's eyes were open, and her nose wasn't even squished, so I knew she really wasn't into it. Anyone knows you almost end up breaking your nose when you kiss someone you like. I slid behind the door, not wanting to be seen.

OMG, what was he thinking? Obviously, like all Earth mawls, he wasn't thinking with the brain between his ears. How could he two-time my BFF Nicola?

I couldn't let this happen. What is it with Ralb?

He fell for Suzz as soon as his butt hit Earth, the one femawl in Bedrocktown who was evil, and I'm not making it up either. She was so mean, so vicious, and so jealous she was a total sociopath. Yes, it was an Earth word I was proud of—the sad thing was I had to learn it firsthand, but I digress.

He'd made a clean break with Suzz and escaped almost *scoth-free*, so why would he want to go back down that rocky road again? He was sure to be hit by a

Mack truck, even if it was wearing a skin-tight spacesuit.

I coughed, but they were so into their face sucking Ralb either didn't hear or was totally ignoring me. I coughed again and again, but I was ignored. Finally, I had a fit like I was hacking up a fur ball, and they stopped. I was startled when Suzzy looked over Ralb's shoulder in my direction, surely, she couldn't hear my praying mantis cough but with the stealthiness I didn't know I possessed, I ducked back behind the door with only my head poking into the room. Then with a hand clamped tighter than a muscle man (I know this because I saw the mark her fingers left) on the outside of his spacesuit, she turned to smirk at the camera before pulling his head back toward her collagen-plumped lips. Hey, those lips were in every tabloid for the past two weeks, and they're a lot bigger than they were in Bedrocktown. Same with her chest, but I'm giving her the benefit of the doubt and crediting a push-up bra and not cosmetic surgery.

I had to think he was taking one for the team, maybe just to get his picture in the tabloids and not enjoying the kiss as much as he was letting on.

I tapped my mandible impatiently. Come on! How long could they hold their breath? It was like they were going for some kind of world record and I was supposed to be the witness. Well, I had newspaper for them. I was not about to waste my time while they stood there locking lips. If they weren't concerned about getting strapped into their seats, well, I was. And if there were only a couple of seats, then in my opinion it was a case of first come, first served. A game of cosmic musical chairs if you will. Basically, a case of you smooch, you lose.

"Umm, Ralb, I hate to interrupt," I said, hostility in my tone as I telepathed him. "Can I chat with you for a minute?"

"Can't you see I'm a little busy right now?" Ralb telepathed back as he broke away from Suzzy's clutches. "What is it you want? You always have to wreck every intimate moment I have."

My mouth dropped open in disbelief. How could he say anything of the sort? He was the one who threw salt water on Josh and me, causing Josh to shape-shift into a resident of Zorca-twenty-three, which started him on the slippery slide to being stepped on by the femawl who was now re-applying lip gloss. Apparently, she was able to keep a tube in a very, and I mean very, tight spacesuit.

I heard Rotsen's sigh, and from the change in Ralb's demeanor he did too.

"Thanks for waiting. Always knew I could count on you, bro." Sarcasm dripped from my tone like the wax from a candle. "I'm telling our Parental Beings."

"I didn't have a choice. Besides, I came back and you weren't there." He shrugged his shoulders. "There was nothing I could do."

"Gawd, if I had a dollar for every time I heard that one, I'd be a millionaire on this planet and Zorca-twenty-three."

He shrugged again. "Looks like you made it without my help anyway."

"Probably because I'm used to it."

"Can we save this bickering until we get home?" Rotsen telepathed to us. "You're both giving me a petal ache."

Oblivious to everything other than herself, Suzzy pulled out a mirror to check her makeup. A mascara wand appeared in her hand, and she flittered it around her eyes like a firefly buzzing a bright light.

"Umm, Ralb, I think we have to get going." She popped a stick of her brand-name gum into her mouth and began to chew like a cow.

I really can't stand someone who chews gum or any kind of food with their mouth open.

"We have to get suited up."

They were standing there sucking each other's molars out while Rotsen and I had been struggling to get on board with Josh. Both of them were so self-centered.

"Okay, enough," I hissed and raised my fists like a welterweight. I don't think I have to tell you how fed up I was with this chick. She was a major pain in the butt. She'd stepped on my mawl without caring for a minute. I so wanted to take her out. And him too.

Beau's voice floated through the air like a balloon. "Suzzy, we need you down here, STAT!"

"Be right back, lover boy," Suzzy cooed.

I bit the inside of my mouth until I tasted blood as we watched her perky butt climb the steps. When she was finally out of sight, I used my pent-up anger. I tried to fly up to his face, but found I was lopsided with my injured wing, the flight taking me toward the door to the left rather than the right. I skittered up over his shoe and found skin by his ankle and sunk my pinchers in hard.

"Ouch. Rotsen, make her stop." Ralb tried to swat me away.

"That was for Nic, what on earth were you thinking

kissing Suzzy? You could catch something lethal. You are such a creep," I spat out, pummeling him again and again. "So much for sibling loyalty." For good measure, I hit him again. Now don't get me wrong, I don't condone violence in any form, but I think you'll agree with me it's justified in this case. "And what about Nicola?"

"What are you talking about?" He shrugged his shoulders, and to give him his due, didn't rub his leg even though it was probably turning a bright yellow with bruises as we spoke.

"Oh, never mind. If you can't figure out what you did wrong, I don't have the time or the patience to explain it to you." I leaned against the door, the fight momentarily draining from me.

"That's why I was kissing her; I was trying to get her to give me some time so I could go back and get you." I knew he was a liar head, but I was impressed he'd come up with an answer so fast.

"Yeah right! If that's the reason, then I'm Elvern."

"Well, you could possibly be," Rotsen piped up. "I've been reading up on the phenomenon, and Elvern has been spotted everywhere from Toronto to Vegas. And don't forget that on his tombstone his name is spelled wrong. Hello, proof enough Elvern is alive."

Ralb and I paused, and I shot Rotsen a major look of disdain.

Once again Ralb shrugged his shoulders, like he didn't have a care in the world. "I really don't know. You always claim to be the brains in the family, so brain away."

"Ralb, time to come and get helmeted up."

Ralb glanced over his shoulder as the whine

traveled down the staircase like a tidal wave, engulfing us all.

"I've really got to go." He leaned over and kissed my cheek. "See you later. I'm sure you'll be fine. You'll figure something out."

Without a backward glance, he climbed the next spiral staircase two at a time.

"Really." Rotsen coughed. "What did you expect?"

"Exactly! I shouldn't be surprised, but I'm always shocked at how shallow he is." I bit my lower lip. "Rotsen, what the heck are we going to do?" Okay, I admit it. I was flip-flopping from being totally ticked off at my brother to utter despair.

Those little holes at the corner of my eyes filled with salt water. "Rotsen, I just wanna go home."

"Okay, Oas, get a grip." Rotsen once again was the voice of responsibility. "Let's go back downstairs with the animals and the cages. When we get there, we'll open your *hanaglug* and figure out what we have to work with."

"What is with all the animals?" I couldn't help but ask.

"I overhead Suzzy say they were for authenticity purposes."

We stole downstairs, ignoring the riotous laughter and chatter drifting from two floors above.

Wiping my drippy nose on the back of my elbow, I did as he suggested. I opened the mid-sized case. A wail escaped me as I spied Josh. When we got back to Zorca-twenty-three, I'd call in all the favors I could. I'd pull a Ralb and kiss up to everyone and everything that could help us. We'd try the experimental drugs and operations that our planet is known across three solar systems and the Milky Way. Josh would live or I'd die trying to save him.

Dang it, we would survive.

"Oas, you're about to die."

Chapter 21

Rotsen's words stopped me dead in my tracks, so to speak.

Calmly, as if he hadn't just told me the world as I know it was about to end, he continued. "You have to go into a cryogenic state or you're going to die."

"That's nonsense," I said firmly. "I came down through the black hole; the atmospheric changes did nothing to me. I'll be fine."

He shrugged his leaves. "You won't be fine. The reason you survived the changes on the way down was due to the fact you morphed from an ananoid to a human, so the humanoid handled the changes, you won't be able to in your current state unless you cryogenic yourself."

I tried to shift one of the cages to make room for me to sit, but they were all chained to the table. As a last resort, I sank down to the cold metal floor and cautiously lifted Josh out and sat him beside me. It gave me extra confidence to have him near—an extra boost I needed right now. Anything and everything I was going through was for the two of us, not just for me.

"Check your *hanaglug*, there might be something in there to help you." Rotsen wrapped his stem around my semi-amputated wing and patted me soothingly.

Remembering the task at hand, I dived back into my *hanaglug*. How were a bottle of pills, a couple of rocks I'd brought for souvenirs, two bobby pins, and a fishing net with more holes than a pair of Ralb's socks (but I must admit the net was smelling sweeter) going to get me home in one piece without my brain exploding and my insides turning to dust? I mean for cripes sake, I wasn't MacGruber.

I snapped the case shut in frustration. "Rotsen, there's absolutely nothing in there that might help me. And it looks like nothing out here either."

"Okay, I'm looking at your perfecto opportunity right now," Rotsen said, grinning at me. "Elementary, my dear Oas. It's really quite simple, so I'm surprised you don't grasp how we can accomplish the unaccomplishable." He crossed his leaves and flashed me an I-know-something-you-don't-know expression. He reached into my *hanaglug* and with his left leaf pulled out a rock and began to scrape equations on the wall. When I saw he was getting into $E=mc^2$ I wanted to smack him.

"I'm only pulling your chain." He smiled, probably in an attempt to get back on my good side. "All you have to do is pop one of those pills, it will knock you out so you can sleep the whole way, and we're GtoG."

"How is taking an iron supplement going to knock me out?

Chapter 22

I held up my hand to stop whatever comment was about to spew forth from his no-mind mind. "Before you say anything, I've never used any. Fortunately, the occasion never arose for me to start taking them. I only had them in case with all the time-traveling it did a number on my system, but I toughed it out." I paused when I saw his raised petals. "Fine, don't believe me. I really don't care one way or the other, but can we get back to how I'm going to remain on the spaceship without anyone seeing me? Frankly, I've had it with Ralb."

"Here, take this!" He pulled a small pill from somewhere in his petals as he slid around from my neck in a fluid motion and undid the door of the nearest cage. "You'll be fine. With the coldness in here and the pill, you'll be asleep in no time, and your Zorcan-twenty-three body will be prepared for the worse."

"So, Alvin, are we cleared for takeoff?" It was Beau's voice on the other side of the door. I could smell his aftershave, the scent wrapping around me like a warm hug.

"Sure are, Mr. Richardson!" Alvin replied. "I've loaded the penguins on, adjusted the temperature so they won't activate during the trip, and we're ready for lift off."

"Good, don't want those annoying creatures

hopping around down here, might throw off the balance of the ship." Beau wacked Alvin on the back as they stepped inside the room and closer to me. "Hey, by the way, you didn't happen to see Ralb's sister in the area, tonight did you?"

I saw Alvin scratch his chin from my hiding spot inside the cage, the pills making me a little drowsy. "I don't know what she looks like, but no one was here who shouldn't be. Why, is she a Suzzy groupie?"

"Yeah, you could say that." Even I could tell there was forced laughter in Beau's voice. "I just thought she might have come by to say goodbye."

"Maybe they aren't that close. I know if my brother Calvin was going up in space, I wouldn't come to say my farewells; I'd be home cleaning out his room so I could move straight in and good riddance. What did she look like?"

"A gorgeous redhead with a drop-dead body."

Yikes, did he mean me? Flattered, I waited for him to continue—not that I was waiting for compliments or anything. I wasn't conceited like Suzzy. Even so, I held my breath and waited for him to continue.

"She was definitely a one-of-a-kind keeper." He shook his head as if ridding it of my memory. "Have the cameras and paparazzi photographed inside here yet?"

"No, I guess they probably got tied up on the gangplank outside, but I'll let a few chosen ones inside when you say so, and they can photograph you three in your seats ready for lift off." Alvin adjusted his tie. "No worries there, sir. Why don't you go on up and get ready yourself? Then when it's time for the photo op you'll be all suited up and ready to go."

"Think I will, think I will." Beau glanced around,

and we locked eyes for a moment, though he of course didn't know it was me.

Maybe it was just my wishful thinking, but Beau seemed a tad sad I wasn't around.

If he only knew.

****

I surveyed my new surroundings, and while it wasn't a four-star hotel, it would suffice. If I moved to the other side, I'd be out of reach of the neighboring monkey who kept reaching through the bars. The floor was lined with shavings, maybe not as comfortable as where stupid Ralb was, but I had the advantage of not having Suzzy in the immediate vicinity.

Cageless butterflies floated through the air, their multifaceted colored wings creating an inside rainbow. My stomach rumbled with the thought of chewing down on one, but drowsiness took over…

I skittered across the enclosure and settled back into the wood chips ready for take-off, my *hanaglug* with Josh inside tucked in beside me like a security blanket from home.

It was then I realized we weren't alone.

I knew Rotsen was sharing quarters with Josh and me. I finally found him hanging on a perch preening himself as he looked into a mirror.

Great! The only cages I'd ever seen with mirrors contained birds. Normally I'd enjoy sharing my quarters with a parrot or cockatoo for the duration of our trip, though their repetitive words might become a tad annoying. But in my current state, I might become a light snack. On the other hand, it might be fun and entertaining to teach the bird some bad words that might come in handy somewhere along the road. I sat back on my hindquarters contemplating the sentences I could teach it. "Suzz is a witch, Suzz is a witch." I'd train the bird to say it for the cameras, and if it came out with a B instead of a W, well, I so could not be held responsible.

Something rustled from under the woodchips in our cage. The smell reminded me of a hamster's cage, but surely space wasn't so cramped they'd put more than one animal to a cage. It would cause all kinds of problems. Animals might eat each other, or they might spend their time on the flight procreating an entirely new species.

Curious I shifted over closer to Rotsen and nudged him off his perch to get his attention.

"Would you stop being such a bully?" Rotsen fumed. "I'd just arranged my petals in an attractive manner and now I have to start all over again."

"Umm, Rotsen, when you opened this cage door for us to hide in, did you happen to read the sign on the cage to see which one we were actually getting into?" I asked keeping an eye on the rustling woodchips. I could make out two eyes peeping from the top of the debris, but the rest of the creature's body was camouflaged. Okay, let's think this through. Something brown was over there, obviously the color of wood shavings. Nothing too vicious was that shade, unless you counted grizzly bears, and that wasn't too likely in this small cage. Unless it was an experimental bear—a mini grizzly the size of a gummy bear—the kind that they could do tests on. Nah, couldn't be.

"What?" Rotsen asked as he inched back onto his perch. "What's got your panties in a bunch now?"

"Rotsen, we're not alone in this cage," I whispered

not wanting to aggravate this sleeping giant under the woodchips. Okay, with its eyes on bright alert, obviously it wasn't snoozing, but either way I didn't want to tick it off until I knew what I was dealing with. I didn't want to become someone's tasty morsel before take-off or liftoff or whatever the heck the proper term is.

"Yeah, well, you never were one to make friends easily." He bent over from his perch and wiped the chips away, causing our cage neighbor to rear its ugly head.

"Oh no," Rotsen panted, scooting back out of reach of the humongous jaws snapping open and shut, in quick succession. He whipped around through the bars and peeked at the sign, his petals turning a pale shade of white.

"What does the sign say?" I asked. In all my years of knowing him, I'd never seen him so white, so scared, and so nervous.

"Umm, sorry, I don't read Latin." He paused. "But I'm sure it's nothing to worry about."

"You are such a lousy liar."

"I'll help in any way I can." He back-petaled around the bars.

"Rotsen, get over to the door and unlock it." I tried to keep eye contact with the monster so my partner could stealthily move to the door. Flipping around through the bars, Rotsen tried to pull up the latch but was unsuccessful. The clanking, clanging, and metal on metal clashing as he jiggled the latch all to no avail.

With all my shifting I was smaller than my regular size of ten decimeters, and with all the pizza in my system, I couldn't fit through the bars. Dang, I knew pizza was bad news.

"What are you? A nine-inch weakling?"

"Wait here, and I'll go and get Ralb. Don't worry. I'll get help for you." Rotsen scurried down, moving like an inch worm, off the white lab table. He hopped up onto the railing and slithered down, his caterpillar-like moves making his ascent slow and methodical. He was very lazy and only moved when he had to, otherwise he relied on others to be his transportation system.

"Hurry," I begged, finally breaking eye contact with the animal to watch Rotsen. When I turned back around the beast wasn't there. I didn't even hear him move, so where the heck was he? "Rotsen, any guess as to who our neighbor here is?"

"From what I can gather, it's a 6-month-old Chuckwalla lizard." He rushed the words out and it took me a minute or two to process his words.

OMG, did he say Chuckwalla lizard?

I backed against the corner of the pen and looked around for a weapon of some kind to protect myself from this monster—this Chuckwalla, the lizard that likes to have my species for lunch, dinner, and anything in between. Stars above, I wished I hadn't taken that pill. I needed all my wits about me.

Chapter 23

I had to rely on my instincts, my own survival guide to beat him at his own game. If I had to go down, I'd go down fighting. I am femawl, hear me roar. I'm a survivor. Glancing around, I weighed my options as to what I could use to win this battle. Someone had stocked this enclosure with enough food to feed the First Battalion. Like the human rations, the lizard's food was freeze-dried and packaged. Great! They must think the Chuckwalla lizard would use its strong claws to rip apart the foil packages when he got hungry enough. Labeled with the TZZ logo and pictures of various animals, the packets were useless to me, unless I wanted to make him a stew. Someone, probably Alvin, had put fresh vegetables in with the lizard. Carrots lay beside the door alongside corncobs and, for some unknown reason, a dead rat, its limp body lying on its side. Yikes! After seeing a documentary on my *wad* that rats caused bubonic plague and wiped out almost the entire country of England in the Dark Ages, I hated rats.

I sidestepped around the vermin and grabbed the closest thing I could find. Okay, it turned out to be a celery stick, but it could make a great sword, or knife, or if worse came to the inevitable worst, I could always tickle the stupid thing.

"Okay, bring it on." I yelled at the lizard with all the force I could muster from my praying mantis stature. Not the most threatening stance I'm sure, but I had to work with what I had.

"Oas, you have more to fear than being alone with a Chuckwalla lizard, you slutski." Had that voice come from the lizard? A voice I recognized from Zorca-twenty-three one had grated on my nerves big-time when I lived there. A voice that reminded me of two-timing tramps—and she had the nerve to call me a slutski. She stole my mawlfriend from me and then paraded him in front of me.

Yes, Kaj was in the house, and for the first time since she and Gorget became an item we were face-to-face—and it was going to get ugly.

She lunged forward and grabbed the celery, the vegetable disappearing in one bite. The monkey found this hilarious, but I was in shock. What was I going to do? How was I going to survive? I skittered around the enclosure out of her reach and grabbed my *hanaglug*, snapping it open, and as she lunged at me I shoved it between her jaws.

"Say ahh." I snapped the case shut, not realizing the tissue Josh was wrapped in had caught on the snap and was now lying beside the rat.

Unprotected!

Chapter 24

"And so you know what a wuss your sister is, she says to me—and I'm making petal quotes here— 'Did you read the sign before you opened the door of the cage to see what was inside?'" Rotsen's whine was getting nearer. "I mean, come on. It was an emergency. I had to think fast, think under pressure, to get her relaxed enough to take the pill and out of harm's way."

"Yeah, well, you know what she's like," Ralb said. "Everything is a major drama with our little diva."

I heard him clomping down the steps like an elephant.

"I honestly don't know where she gets it from! Probably something to do with having so many brothers and sisters, she has to do something, anything to get attention. I think you'll agree she's a major attention seeker, anything to get someone to turn a speck of awareness in her direction and she's happy as a pig in a poke."

"Totally agree," Rotsen said. "I really don't know how you put up with her all those years. Mate, you certainly deserve a medal."

"Would you two shut up," I said, not taking my eyes off Kaj. I knew if I did I would be a dog's breakfast, or rather a lizard's dinner. Anyway, she could get the jump on me. She would and wouldn't think twice about it. My *hanaglug* would only last so long. It wasn't built to be a lizard slayer.

"Now, now. I wouldn't get testy if I were you, little sis," Ralb said. "From where I'm standing, I'm holding all the cards in this situation and you, dear sis, are behind bars where you no doubt belong sharing company with that cute little lizard."

"That cute little lizard is Kaj."

"Really. So now you're going to tell me you're in a cage with a lizard who's none other than your worst enemy?" Ralb snorted. "You certainly are the funny one."

"I'm not kidding, you jerk. I don't know how she did it, but she got down here and changed into this despicable, young, ugly beast."

"I think you've inhaled too much spaceship exhaust." Rotsen laughed. "Look, if it was Kaj she'd speak. Look at the dumb creature. It's just staring at the bars."

"Come on, Kaj, show them it's really you." I didn't want them to think I was any crazier than they already did. Then it hit me like a two-by-four straight to the old noggin. Of course, she wouldn't show her stripes, so to speak. She wouldn't admit she was who she was, because if she admitted it Rotsen and Ralb would get me out of there so fast her head would spin. Oh no, my arch enemy would keep silent. She really was an evil villain, a major horrible insect/lizard. She wanted to toy with me, to toss me around like a cat with a mouse, a lion with an antelope, a dog with a bone. Yes, I was meant to be played with, and obviously once again I'd have to rely on my intuition to save the day, not to mention my life.

"Rotsen, you're right. I made it all up about Kaj." I

yanked my *hanaglug* from her stinky jaws and banged it against the millimeter-distanced bars like I was a prisoner on death row. The monkey in the next cage reached out to grab it, but I tug-of-warred it out of his reach. I needed to keep all the weapons I could find.

"See, *major drama queen.*" Rotsen high-fived Ralb. "So, what do you say we go back up to where our little Suzzy is purring?" Rotsen climbed up to Ralb's shoulder and sat there as content as a parrot.

"Sure thing. Do you think from the little bit you saw of us together she's into me?" Ralb bent over and preened in the reflective aluminum of a satellite meant to be added to the Space Port so the astronauts could play video games. Frankly, it kind of perturbed me. Here I was a hard-working taxpayer—okay, I would be if I worked and paid taxes—and the government is wasting money like it grows on trees, which I know for a fact it doesn't on your planet. Zorca-twenty-three, however, is another story. You should see the size of our money trees. They drip with coins, bills, and on one special tree that my Parental Beings happen to own, the equivalent of one of your thousand-dollar bills. Have you seen the color of our money? It has more colors than a peacock and, if you ask me, it's way prettier.

"She's totally into you, man," Rotsen said. "I've never seen anyone more eager to jump into your head."

"Hello!" I called out. "I'm in here with the predator from H-E-double-hockey-sticks and you two are chick talking." I paused to catch my breath; I was so furious. "Is there any way you could get me out of here, and then you can go back to your honey?"

"Actually," Rotsen said. "According to the manual I was reading about safe landings and take-offs, the most secure place for you to be is inside a bolted down item." He slithered down Ralb's shoulder and picked at the metal bolts chaining the cage to the table. "Yep, this looks pretty darn secure." He walked back up my brother's arm and perched back on him. "So, if I were you, I'd just sit tight and we'll come and get you when we're safely back on Zorca-twenty-three."

I made a last-ditch effort to get help, and I knew the only way to do it would be to tick off Rotsen. "Didn't they say there were no weeds allowed on board?"

I could see his leaves tighten, his stem harden.

"What did you call me?" He was so mad, he didn't even use an accent.

"Never you mind," Ralb answered. "I'll just tuck you here inside my spacesuit and no one will be the wiser."

"So, you guys are just going to leave me here with Kaj?"

"No, I'm going to leave you in there with a baby Chuckwalla lizard. There's lots of packaged food in there, you'll be fine. They don't eat insects."

"Wait," I called to deaf ears as I reluctantly broke eye contact with Kaj and watched them hike back up the stairs, my brother preening the entire way. Totally typical. One would think my bro or at least Rotsen would get me out. I mean, even if they didn't think it was Kaj, my life was still in danger. Cripeola, it wasn't like I was a cat with nine lives.

Once again I had to rely on myself and my brains.

I turned back to face my adversary. Shoot, I had to do something I'd promised myself I'd never, ever, ever in ten thousand light years do.

I had to be nice to Kaj.

Chapter 25

You don't know how much it was going to kill me to do that. I really seriously debated whether I should just let her eat me and be done with it. Surely it was the lesser of two evils. But then I realized I'd never see my Parental Beings again, and I fought back tears. I'd never smell a rose again or hear the sweet sound of a bird. Okay, that one I really wouldn't miss too much because I find some of them really annoying. Like the crowing of a rooster and how they think they're Earth's alarm clock and wake everybody at daybreak. I mean, come on. Haven't they heard you folks have alarm clocks that are a little easier on the system than a bird waking you out of a dead sleep?

Then I heard rustling in the woodchips, louder and closer.

"Okay, Kaj, make it fast." I closed my eyes and waited for the impact of her jaws on my torso.

Nothing.

I waited and still nothing.

I opened one eye lid a slit, and then the other. She was sitting across the cage watching me. I knew in martial arts you always waited for your opponent to make the first move and then used their moves against them, but what if your opponent doesn't make a move?

"Why are you toying with me?" I cringed. I never was a big fan of hide and seek. I hated being the hider. I could never sit still long enough to be found or I'd start laughing at the most inopportune time. Then on the flip side, I equally didn't like having to find people. It all seemed kind of pointless in the long run. Who really cared? If you had a really good spot, no one could find you, and the game became really boring. I'd much rather sit outside with a good book and my *wad* listening to the latest from Peach Acid. I tell you that band really rocks.

Again, she didn't answer me. She continued to glare at me with her unblinking stare that was getting on my nerves. It was extremely difficult to have a staring contest with a creature that didn't have eyelids.

"Come on, Kaj. What's the matter? Lizard's got your forked tongue?" I stalked up and danced in front of her, trying to taunt her into moving, into doing anything. I debated with myself and finally decided to poke her.

I jabbed my front legs, which I normally use for grasping, as if I were a boxing kangaroo. Of course, she didn't move an inch. For whatever reason, she was playing dead, and frankly I couldn't be happier.

I let down my guard and trotted happily over to the water bowl, where I inhaled a long lap of liquid.

"You really are a stupid creature, aren't you?" Kaj whispered so quietly I was almost sure I had imagined it. "Please explain to me why Gorget loves you and not me?"

Okay, sometimes I'm not the smartest alien in the solar system, and I wanted to take back the words the minute I said them. "Are you crazy?"

"He told me he couldn't be with me because he still loved you." Kaj spit the words out, her red tongue looking indeed like she was breathing fire.

"That's crazy." Stars, what is it with me and those stupid words? "He broke up with me to go out with you."

"He told me he loves your independence, likes how you're a free spirit. I talked to Zen, and he warned me not to come, but I couldn't stay on Zorca-twenty-three and listen to Gorget go on and on about how wonderful you are. I got a ticket at the Black Hole Market and headed down. How was I to know I'd shape shift into a lizard? What a frigging mess my life has turned out to be. Why doesn't Gorget love me?"

Mawls, what is it with them? I'll never understand it. "He told me if I came to Earth, it was over between us. He just wants what he can't have." I paused. "Kaj, he's a loser!"

Oh no, I overstepped my boundaries.

I felt a warm breath on the back of my neck and cringed. Even from this distance, I could smell the evil odor emanating from her. Obviously, this creature has never heard of a toothbrush or even a tongue brush. My hackles rose, and I prepared myself for the inevitable.

I was going to join Josh in the afterlife.

I was going to die.

Chapter 26

"Let's fly to Zorca-twenty-three, I'll show you my planet for freeeeeee." Rotsen's musical voice traveled down the stairs. "Kaj, if you lay one dirty claw on her, I'll find the guns they have hidden on board here and I'll shoot."

Kaj's head whipped around behind me, the breeze causing several of the wood chips to flutter like bulrush seeds in the air.

"Stay out of this, Rotsen, it doesn't concern you. This is between me and Oas," she said. "Back off or I'll come after you as well when I finish with this tramp."

"Hey, who are you calling a tramp?" I could only stand so much from this thorn in my side. "You were the one who stole Gorget from me! Or I should say, you were the one who moved in on my major cast-off after I was done with him." I paused for dramatic effect. "So really, I don't hold any grudge and should be thanking you for picking up my trash."

"Why you little…." She stormed toward me, the cedar chips flying around the cage like a tornado.

But I was prepared.

Before I had time to think about what I was doing, to avoid inhaling the rotting rat, I picked it up by the tail with my front legs and swung it around like I was a discus thrower. When I had enough momentum, I let go and let it clock her right in the noggin. Stunned, she

135

dropped her head down, shaking it as if to rid it of cobwebs.

Rotsen sprung open the door to the cage, and I leaped through, slamming the door behind me.

Oh crapola! As the door sprung shut, I realized my *hanaglug* was sitting in the corner of the cage. I ignored it, hoping Kaj wouldn't notice it either. I'd come back and get it when we landed on Zorca-twenty-three. Josh's body, wrapped in the tissue, had been flung onto the other side of the cage, out of sight hidden under the shavings.

"Take that Kaj!" I boosted one leg up into the air in victory. "You should know better than to mess with the best."

She shook her head, her words coming out slow and slurred. "Just wait, you little witch. I'll get you, sooner or later."

"Yeah, you and who's army?" I smirked, now I was safe on the other side of the bars I felt free to taunt her all I wanted. "I have to find out, how did you end up here?"

"Gorget says he still loves you," she said, sounding like a two-year-old on her way to a major tantrum. "But let's just say, they are turning me loose when we get to the Space Port and you will not be safe."

"Yeah, well, sticks and stones, baby, sticks and stones." I giggled in glee. "For now, I'm here and you're there. And enjoy that rat," I said. "I heard they cause bubonic plague, so bon appetite."

"Wow, remind me never, ever to get on your wrong side." Rotsen laughed.

"Did you check out any good hiding spots for us?" I asked, suddenly exhausted by the events of the night.

It was hard to believe it had only been a few short hours ago that I'd landed on the red carpet at the TZZ's. Now I had to cramp myself into some kind of hidey-hole while Ralb got to recline in the lap of luxury for the entire trip. How is it my bro always ended up on his feet, whereas I ended up usually on my butkis?

"There's one really good one, but I'm afraid you're not going to like it very much," Rotsen whispered when we'd finally reached the top step.

In front of us, Ralb was sandwiched between Beau and Suzzy, wedged in the middle seat like a sardine in a can. Frankly, now I'd seen the conditions of his travels, I wouldn't have traded with him, especially since it would mean being crammed in by Suzzy, and worse, Beau. The man really got under all my layers of skin. I don't care if he's a good kisser—Josh, may he rest in peace, could have learned a few things. But Beau was a major pain in the butkis and nothing, and I mean nothing, he could do would impress me.

I stopped just outside the door as I heard their voices.

"Hey, Ralb, does your hot sister have a boyfriend?" Beau asked, poking Ralb with a sequined glove, reminding me of a certain pop star.

"Yeah right. That's a good one." Ralb flipped up the shield of his helmet and grinned. "Have you spent any time with her? If you did, you'd know no one could put up with her for any length of time."

"Are you kidding me? She's a totalable babe."

Totalable babe! What kind of description is that? I do have a mind you know, and I am a fan of Shakespeare. Okay, I know his work isn't too popular with high school students, but the man had a way with words. Okay, fine. I admit, he could have summarized his sentences a bit and not dragged on about daggers before me, etc. But if you read his plays for the words, I'm sure you'd agree with me the words are just like poetry.

"Are you sure we're talking about the same sister? I do have more than one, you know." Ralb grinned again, the smile I always wanted to whip off his face with something rough.

"Hello, can someone help me over here?" Suzzy said, sucking on one of her fingers like a baby. She'd caught her nail on the outside of her glove, causing the nail to break below the quick. I wasn't without sympathy since I'd done that myself and it is painful, but I mean, suck it up, beautiful, you're about to space travel and a ripped nail will be the least of your troubles.

"Oh, sure thing, Suzzy." Ralb reached over, yanked her finger, and popped it into his own mouth, the sucking noise reminding me of a mosquito feasting.

Suzzy's suit had her sponsors' logos covering her bits, and TZZ logos strategically placed around a diagram of the solar system. The suit was molded to her frame and even with the extra padding and fire-retardant material only inflated her to a size six. I saw her smoothing down the extra stuffing as she glanced toward Ralb to see if he'd noticed her.

I was about to gag. I bent over to try and keep my dinner down. I didn't even realize I had anything left in my stomach after the last episode, but my stomach contents spewed up and I did vomit a bit of grass and pizza.

Rotsen patted my back, and I soon got over my

queasiness, but I would have given my left arm for a sip of carbonated soda. "Okay. I'm okay," I said. "Now, where are we going to hide?"

"Well, I found two spots for us, and I'm afraid you're not going to be impressed by either one."

"Hit me with your best shooter," I said while watching Beau. He was playing with his watch, pushing and pulling buttons and knobs. It took me a couple of minutes to realize he was playing a video game and not mesmerized by the time.

"Hey, Suzzy, Ralb. I just beat the highest level of Space Monsters. How good am I?" He pumped his arm in the air. "I just creamed someone whose online name is AprilOAS23. What kind of lame screen name is that?"

I had to bite my lips to quit from yelling out. I was AprilOAS23, and it wasn't like I worked hard at getting to the level. I did it in my spare time. I did it while I was watching television on my *wad* at home—it wasn't exactly brain surgery.

"Yeah, it is pretty lame," Ralb agreed when he finally removed Suzzy's finger from his mouth. "I'm glad to see someone beat her."

"Do you know AprilOAS23?" Beau asked, with more curiosity than the matter deserved.

"Nah, I sure don't." Ralb settled back into his seat. "Do either of you have any idea when this flight takes off?"

"We're waiting for the cameramen to shoot our pics for the tabloids," Beau said without glancing up from his watch.

"Should be any time now," Suzzy said, picking up a clipboard and reading the charts. She flipped a page over and read. "The flight is supposed to take seventy-two hours, which is a long time for the human body to remain sedated. Now if you'd please open the top compartment of your armrest, you will find each one contains three capsules."

I listened and watched as robot-like each of the three travelers lifted the lids on the padded armrests and fingered the packages.

"Okay, I have mine," Ralb said. "There's a red one, a white one, and a yellow one. Which one are we supposed to take when we take off?"

"Just a second." Suzzy moved a finger along the page as she read. "The yellow tablet is for stomach upset and should be taken with plenty of water up to thirty minutes before take-off. Travel will become somewhat tipsy-turvy."

"Don't you mean *topsy*, not *tipsy*?" Beau asked, laughing. "Unless we're taking it with some hard alcohol, I hope I'm not tipsy!"

Uh-oh! Even I knew Suzzy didn't like being the butt of any jokes.

"Beau, it's obviously a typo and by the by, when we get back to Earth, you are so fired."

"Uh, right. Sorry, Suzzy," Beau said. "Please go on. Does it say anything about Black Holes?"

I could tell him a thing or two about them. Like the last time I traveled through one, I ended up with cool clothes and Peddy Bundt hair. But I wanted to hear the "official" version, or I should say the Earthling version.

"Black Holes are like an enormous vacuum cleaner, the clean-up commander of space. Scientists can't really tell what they are or what they look like because they're black, but from the debris that's sucked into their core, we can tell they're pretty intense and not to be toyed with." She stopped reading and began to suck her index finger. "Crap! I hate it when I get a paper cut."

I don't know if they dumbed down the words for her or not, but it didn't sound like a very professional, space-quality document. Usually, scientific documents contained words with more letters than the entire alphabet.

"Okay, so whoever is driving this boat, er, ship, stay away from the holes."

Ralb opened his mouth to add something to Beau's comments but stopped himself for once. "Please go on, Suzzy."

"Anyone got a bandage?" she asked. At this rate, she was going to be the reigning Whine Queen of all space. Maybe I should send her down to Kaj, and they could bond and complain away together.

Suck-up Ralb handed her one from the breast pocket of his jumpsuit and even peeled the paper off it.

"Rotsen, what are we going to do? Where are we going to stay?" I asked, suddenly realizing we were out in the open and vulnerable to attack, provided any of padded-marshmallow passengers could move. "What are our choices again?"

"I never did get around to telling you. You were mesmerized by Beau beating your score at Space Monsters." He held up his left leaf. "Before we go that route again, I want you to listen carefully to each of our options and weigh each of the choices before you make a decision. It's a long flight, and I don't want to have you turning into Suzzy and complaining the entire way."

"Fine! When have you ever heard me...oh, never mind." I knew I was fighting a losing battle. We'd be going around and around like a hula hoop if I didn't get us situated. I peeked over his petals to see where we might secure ourselves and shrugged. I couldn't see any obvious place.

Looking like Newton when the apple fell on his head, Rotsen nodded toward Ralb, a smarty pants look on his face. "There's the inside of his armrest."

"Are you kidding me?" I was shocked someone so smart would come up with such a dumb idea. "We'd be trapped and at the mercy of my stupid brother. No way, no how, am I going to climb in there. You know he'd never let us out and we'd suffocate. What's your second idea, Einstein?"

"For some unknown reason, Beau has a different spacesuit than everyone else. If you'd peeled your eyes away from the cleft in his chin, you would have noticed," Rotsen said with a snort.

"I don't have any idea what you're talking about. I was just checking out his helmet because, um, well, it looks like it might not stand up to the stringent conditions of space travel."

"Sure, you were." He folded his leaves and sighed. "Anyhow, if you notice, his spacesuit has extra compartments, and there's an extra-large one on the arm of his left sleeve."

Now that was appealing. Not to give you the wrong idea about me. I mean, I am in mourning for my dear, departed Josh, but I'm sure you'd agree with me, it is a pretty tempting idea to spend the next however many hours cuddled in a down-filled pocket, nice and toasty beside a bulging bicep. Not that I noticed, mind you. I just assumed it would be nice and warm given how space travel is extremely frigid. Besides, it would probably keep me at the correct temperature. I'm just saying.

"I think you're right. Option number two is a lot more appealing than anything to do with Ralb." I yawned.

"Are you sure? I know how you're not really a huge fan of Beau, and well, I wouldn't want to make you uncomfortable. So, give me a minute and let me think. Maybe I can come up with something different."

"No." I rushed to speak. "Follow my lead."

I skittered across the floor and climbed up along the back of the seats, taking care not to be seen. Ralb and Beau were still talking about the pills. My brother was living the life of Riley, lapping up the luxuries of first class, while I was basically in steerage.

"Wow, I can't believe they're only giving us three little tablets for an entire space flight. Doesn't it seem a little skimpy?" Beau asked, sounding a tad nervous.

Chewing on his bottom lip, he didn't even notice when I, a cute little praying mantis, climbed into his pocket. Aww, heaven. Now this was living!

"Nah, we'll likely be conked out for most of the flight." Suzzy laughed. "I heard another major celebrity did the vomit comet as a way to lose weight. Maybe it'll become the latest diet fad in H-wood." She snorted. "Want a great fashion accessory? Try a space rocket! I can see them lining up to follow my lead. Once again, I'll be a major trend-setter, just like when I was the first to wear Jimmy Chingo." She reached into one of her wrist pockets and pulled out enough make-up to fill a department store counter and still have spaces left.

Suzzy applied a layer of foundation, then cover-all, then blush, and then smeared rouge on her cheekbones. Next came the eyes, and I have to say I was mildly impressed. She put on eye shadow—I lost count after three colors—then mascara, and then used an eyelash curler, all this without the aid of a mirror or any other reflective device. Pursing her lips, she applied gloss with the tip of her baby finger.

"Well, boys, how do I look?" Coyly, and with a glance from under her lashes, she fluttered her eyelids at Ralb, ignoring Beau completely. I guess she was still miffed at his earlier comments.

Yes, count on my brother to do a double take. If he didn't watch out, he'd end up in a neck brace, which would more than serve him right.

"Kazooza. I'm sure glad I'm sitting beside you for the duration of the trip," Ralb said as he reached over and took her hand. "You are one hot lady, lady."

"Why don't you two get a room?" Beau echoed what I was already thinking. The smile on Suzzy's face was one I'd seen on a contented cheetah after a successful kill. What is it with these Earth girls who think my brother is so hot he sizzles? Though really who am I to judge you girls? I've been sideswiped by a drooping antenna more than once. Throw in a drooping eyelid, like Gorget's, and I was a goner until I realized what a skunk he was.

"So, what's the rest of the game plan?" Ralb asked as I snuggled deeper into Beau's pocket, carrying Rotsen with me as he twisted around my mantis form to make more room. I accidentally inhaled my host's now-familiar scent. Something about the smell made my stomach swizzle, but in a good way.

"I can answer that one." I poked my head out a tad to see Alvin enter the capsule. He was carrying a mug, the string of a teabag hanging over the side. "We're ready for take-off. Is everyone comfortable and ready to roll?"

Three heads nodded. The demeanor in the room had changed from the laughing, joking, lightheartedness to serious. Reality of the event about to take place seemed to weight the air in the room.

The monitor flashed on, and after thirty seconds of static a head popped up.

"Hi, all, this is Ikey Newton from Mission Control. Now to summarize the itinerary, in about five minutes, the guards are going to let the press in and they'll take the pictures which will likely end up on the Internet"— he glanced down at his watch— "in about ten minutes." He looked at the three passengers. "The lighting in here is good." He shrugged. "Suzzy, will you have enough time to get some makeup on?"

Even I could tell from my vantage point she was seething.

"I'm good." She was like a kettle about to reach its boiling point. She dropped her down-home accent and went with the voice she was born with. "Go on!"

"Alrighty then." Ikey shrugged. "After that, we'll lock you all in here tighter than an oil drum, and you can watch those monitors overhead to see what's going on outside the capsule."

Alvin watched the performance from the door, slurped again, and cursed. "I don't know how many times I have to burn my tongue before I remember to blow on the tea."

He cautiously sipped his tea and continued.

"Before you know it, you'll be tripping the light fantastic and dancing with comets in the sky."

"Alvin, please show them what I briefed you on already about their suits." Ikey ordered.

Alvin put the mug down on the arm of Suzzy's chair and said, "If you take a gander at your spacesuits, you'll notice there are small tubes running around the inside. They contain water to help keep the heat down inside, providing more of a comfort zone."

Each of the occupants shifted slightly as if to feel for the tubes.

Ikey picked up the dialogue. "Your helmets are to be worn upon liftoff and are not to be removed at any time or basically your brain will explode, not to sugar coat it." He laughed. "And believe me, that wouldn't be a pretty sight."

Suzzy squirmed and shifted in her seat, sending the mug flying. Tea covered the entire right side of her spacesuit, and the porcelain smashed on the floor, the sound echoing in the close quarters. Suzzy tried to jump out of her seat, but she'd already fastened her seatbelt and it grabbed her around the stomach. Her face turned red, and her eyes bulged as she fell backward.

Alvin calmly tugged at the safety catch and released the belt. Ignoring her frigid glance, he said, "Another feature they've included is when you are spinning out of control at warp speed, your seatbelt automatically tightens to keep you in position."

I peered toward Beau and noticed he was calm, cool, and collected. He didn't appear nervous. The pills must have kicked in. I had to say I was quite impressed. I was a tad apprehensive, I must admit, and I was a seasoned traveler. I knew how in eight minutes flat we'd be out of the Earth's atmosphere and spinning out of control. This wasn't going to be a tea party, even if there was tea dripping off Suzzy's suit and onto the floor. I opened my mouth to ask if someone was going to clean it up, and then realized I wasn't supposed to be here, so I kept my trap shut. I watched the liquid ballet dance toward the control panel on the floor. Who would design a sixty-million-dollar space vehicle with buttons on the floor? I mean, anyone could step on them, and then we'd be in big trouble.

I'd hate to think what would happen if some kind of hot liquid got in and gummed them all up, but hey, I was just the passenger. I wasn't navigating this adventure. I could just sit back and enjoy the ride and count the hours until I was back home and Josh would be whole once again.

Chapter 27

A knock interrupted Alvin's spiel and as one we glanced towards the source. An enormous black box was shoved through the opening, attached around the neck by a head. The camera men had arrived.

Before we could even speak, flashbulbs sparked like faulty Christmas lights.

"Suzzy, over here!" an accented voice yelled from the doorway, obviously not wanting to squeeze into the tight space. "Let's see you in the cute helmet."

As if she'd recently had an appointment with a top stylist, which I'm sure she had, Suzzy gently placed the no doubt custom-made helmet on her head. The helmet was unlike anything I'd ever seen. The lightly tinted visor covered the entire face and flipped from the bottom upward. The metal of the rest of it wasn't rounded, but rather flat and streamlined with the TZZ logo plastered all over it.

"Okay, folks just a few more shots before take-off." Alvin held up his two fingers, the universal sign for peace as well as the two-minute warning. "And remember all, we will have live video feed, and you'll be able to download pictures from the website that TZZ is graciously sharing for a nominal fee."

I ducked my head back inside Beau's pocket, a sudden headache erupting from the glare and glamour. I so could not be an Earth star along the lines of Suzzy. I didn't have the stomach or the patience for the stage lights. She lapped it up like a cat with a fresh bowl of cream.

You'd think she'd get whiplash the way her head flipped around left and right for the best camera angle. Ralb and Beau might as well have been pillars in the background for all the interest anybody paid them. I do think I was accidentally in one of the photos, though, because of the awkward angle, not that I had planned it or anything.

"Okay, folks, enough pictures." Alvin popped each of the passengers with a fist bump. "Have a great flight, and we'll see you when you land back here." He picked up some of the bigger pieces of his mug and backtracked out the door, pulling it shut behind him.

My mouth dropped open as I listened to the sounds of the ramp moving away. We had no intention of coming back! We were on a one-way mission back to Zorca-twenty-three, even with my brother navigating. I didn't sign up for this fairytale trip to come back to this gosh-forsaken planet. Alvin, these aliens had different plans.

Ralb must have echoed my thoughts because like an episode of *an old television sitcom*, he repeated exactly what I was thinking. "Suzzy, what does he mean come back? I thought we were heading to space and you were continuing on to the Space Port?"

"Well, here's the thing. I wasn't able to get insured to travel past the atmosphere to actually travel to the Space Port." She turned away from the onboard camera and covered the mic in her helmet.

"So where exactly are we going?" Ralb asked, sounding none too pleased.

"Well, you know how there's all the controversial arguments about the original moon landing being faked just so we could say we beat the Russians in space travel?" Ralb nodded, and she continued, and resorting to her country twang once again, "We're all just jetting up past the clouds, then when the coast is clear as a new baby's face"—she glanced around and smiled, then seemed a tad disappointed when the smiles weren't returned— "we come back down and get our pictures taken against a backdrop inside an airplane hangar."

"What a fake!" I blurted out loud.

No one paid any attention to me though as Ralb interrupted her. "So, we're not heading to outer space? We're basically on an airplane ride for publicity?" Ralb asked. "So, what's with the charade?"

I, for one, was impressed he knew such an awesome-sounding French word.

"It's all about publicity, baby." Now Suzzy's accent sounded like a bad rip-off from a spy movie. "Right, Beau?"

"Yeah, right! Sorry to disappoint you, mate."

Okay, Ralb this is when you kick it into high gear and karate chop them all, take over the controls, and away we go.

"So, is this all pretend?" Ralb asked, looking around. "All these buttons and knobs are just props, like we're in some high-tech NASA model?"

"Pretty much."

"And the pills?"

"Placebo," she cooed. "Sugar pills, just for the cameras."

Ikey's smile shone through the monitor. "Now, if everyone is strapped in, we're going to take off in one minute flat." He winked again, and I realized he either thought he was majorly cool or had an astigmatism. Either way the winking was getting on my nerves.

"Just so I get this straight," Ralb said as he tightened his seat belt. "We're going on an amusement park ride, only slightly higher than a rollercoaster, and then heading back down into the desert, where we'll be taken to a building with a mock-up of a planet and the Space Port. Then we'll pretend we're actually on the Space Port? What the heck?"

Ikey smiled again. "What's got his panties in a knot? Anyone should be thrilled to be sitting next to you, Suzzy."

"True, but can we just get the ride on the road? I have to be back in H-wood tonight to read over scripts, which of course no one will know about. There's a motorcade waiting for me that would make the president's look puny." She reached into her pocket and brought out a small tin of lip gloss. Sticking her baby finger into the goo, she flipped up the visor and applied it with the accuracy of a plastic surgeon.

I observed Ralb catching my eye and winking. What is it with these winksters? First the video feed guy and then my brother.

Then it hit me.

Big time.

Ralb was going to get us home. For real, this time.

Chapter 28

"Seatbelt sign is lit up, and all systems are go." Ikey spoke into a 1950s-era microphone that I assumed was part of the set. "Please place your tray tables in an upright position and no smoking."

Beau seemed to be handling the last order okay, and I snuggled deeper into his pocket. When I got home if my plans didn't work and I buried Josh, I'd have a respectable period of mourning, give myself time to really get over him, and then I'd gently get back into the dating scene. But I wasn't ready yet by any stretch of anyone's imagination.

"I'm a little nervous about take-off." Beau punched Ralb in the arm. "Tell me some details about your sister. I'd really like to meet up with her again someday, but to be honest, she is a tad annoying. She even had the nerve to lecture me about smoking, which I know I should quit."

"Believe me, you don't want to have anything to do with her," Ralb said. "Didn't I already go over this with you?"

"Just keep talking. I'm listening."

"She likes the bad boys. She went with a guy from our home plan—er...I mean town who fooled around with every other femawl, er, female and she was too clueless to notice."

"As her brother, why wouldn't you take the guy

out?" Beau asked. "I know if I had a sister, especially one as hot as her, I'd do anything to protect her."

Aww, Beau was quickly earning major points, but I still wasn't interested. Not even slightly, not even a little bit, not even a tad.

"Oas, urr, April is quite capable of looking after herself." He sounded defensive, and I can't say I really blamed him. If he ever did try to defend me, I'd either drop dead from laughing or I'd clobber him myself.

"So, what's with this Josh dude? Is he still in the picture? I haven't seen him hanging around her. And if she was my gal I sure wouldn't let her out of my sight. Was he another bad guy who treated her like crap?"

"He wasn't too bad actually. I kind of got along with him okay," Ralb said. "He was April's first Earth boyfriend, and he was somewhat decent, wanted to be an astronaut before he died and everything."

Ralb, you are a complete idiot. You just admitted I had an *Earth* boyfriend. Are you nuts? Crazy! I tried to telepath to him to shut up and quit talking about me before he spilled the beans that we were all aliens.

Luckily Beau didn't pick up on the one word I was worried about but rather the other one that stood out.

"So, this Josh dude is dead?"

"Yeah, died at the TZZ awards show. He had a misadventure with a shoe, and his soul is now on its way to Heaven." If I'd been closer to Ralb, I would have decked him for that. Who was he to make fun of my personal tragedy? And yes, I got his idiotic pun about the soul and shoe joke.

"Wow, an astronaut, he must have been really smart," Beau said, sounding dejected. "I must have been so busy keeping Suzzy on the red carpet that I didn't hear any sirens."

"Yeah, well, I think we were inside the auditorium when it happened," Ralb said, "but getting back to Josh, I'm sure you could beat him in a game of wits. He was book smart but not too street smart if you know what I mean." Ralb's head jerked around as Suzzy unzipped her jumpsuit even farther.

"Guys, can we please get off the topic of Ralb's boring sister and her even more boring love life?" She laughed. "Beau, she's not even here, and if she was I'm sure she wouldn't give you the time of day." She lowered the zipper along with Ralb's eyes as they followed every move. "Besides, I could tell you are totally not her type. There are girls who go for nice, clean cut guys and girls who go for thugs, and she was definitely the latter."

I so didn't get why she was dissing Josh. They'd grown up in the same town, and if not really friends, they should have each other's backs. Then it hit me like a meteorite. He wouldn't give her the time of day, night, or anything else. He was a gazillion times smarter than Ralb.

"Thanks, Suzzy. I think." Beau sank back in his seat and intertwined his fingers. "I guess you're right. I probably never would have stood a chance with her. Not because of what you said, but because she seemed like the type of girl who wouldn't be impressed by who I know or how I could launch her career. She's the type who generally likes people for themselves." He sighed. "Do you know how hard it is to find a person in this town who's genuine and not a phony baloney?"

"Hello, you're sharing space with one right now," Suzzy said.

It took me a minute to realize she wasn't referring to me being in his pocket, but to herself.

"Now how about holding my hand, Ralb?" she said, snapping her fingers, flipping her mic back on.

"Remember as well," Ikey said with a smirk. "Our onboard camera will be recording your every move, your every facial expression and, of course, your conversation, so keep it clean folks. We've got a live feed, so Suzzy's fans will be able to access it on her website."

"Great, and I'll be blogging as well," Suzzy said, her mini laptop in her hand as she typed. Personally, I don't know how she managed it, clutching Ralb's hand at the same time, but then I was relieved to see her fasten the laptop down with straps. We definitely didn't want any flying projectiles in the capsule.

The countdown started. "Five…four…three…two…one…*blast off.*" As Ikey hit the final words, the capsule began to vibrate, the tremors reverberating across the floor. Comparing it to an earthquake would give the quake too much credit. The pieces from the mug slid across the floor as the rocket separated from its supports. A combination of gas, peroxide, and for some reason cinnamon filled my nostrils, and I struggled to breathe. I forget how involved space travel is for you Earthlings. On Zorca-twenty-three all we have to do is hop on the fastest passing asteroid and voila we're space-bound. No preparation, no ungodly smells turning my stomach.

Something was digging into my side in Beau's pocket. I sunk deeper inside and was relieved to find it was a foil-wrapped piece of Suzzy's brand of gum. Chewing gum always seemed to settle my nerves and stomach contents, so I assumed it wouldn't be any different now. Well, I don't know about you, but there's a famous saying on Zorca-twenty-three, the word "assume" makes a you know what out of you and me.

Oh snap! Using my antenna, I unwrapped the gum and popped it into my mouth as a burst of flavor flooded inside, causing my mouth to clamp shut and my nostrils to flare, and in a totally not good way. A familiar tang hit my taste buds, and I realized—too late—I was in bad shape.

The buttery, salty taste popped through all my senses. I loved the tanginess. I'd never experienced popcorn until I hit Earth, but like a lot of Earth things, it didn't agree with my system. Kind of like cheese to a lactose intolerant Earthling—that was what I was experiencing. Stomach aches rolled through me, ten times worse than the G-forces I'd experienced at lift off. My head pounded like drums from an angry warlord intent on starting a major battle.

But even worse than that was something I never imagined, never expected to experience any time soon.

I was starting to morph into a human.

Inside Beau's pocket.

Chapter 29

With superpower skills I didn't know he possessed, Rotsen flipped out of Beau's pocket and dove onto Ralb's helmet, snaking his way inside.

With petal to my brother's eye, he blocked his view so Ralb had nowhere else to look. "Ralb, you have to help Oas," he yelled.

"What is her problem now?" Ralb asked, his voice echoing through the mask. Luckily the sound of the engines was blocking out his voice to all but me and Rotsen.

"You've got to help her. She's starting to Zorca change."

"Yeah, right. Tell me another one." Ralb laughed. "Rotsen, her drama queenness is wearing off on you. You know that would only happen when certain conditions are met, and she hasn't had popcorn, so bug off and leave me alone."

"Rotsen!" I telepathed in panic mode, like rapid-fire Morse code. "You have to do something to distract them. I can't be seen getting out of Beau's pocket; it will totally gross them out."

Of course, Ralb being Ralb did the first thing that came to his pea-sized brain. He ripped me out of Beau's pocket and threw me like he was an NFL quarterback.

"What the heck, man?" Beau asked, his eyes highlighting his shock.

"I thought you had a bug on you," Ralb said before turning his attention back to Suzzy.

I had to admit I was freaking out. I felt like my fingers were on fire, stretching and cracking as they changed from mantis to human shape, the bones splitting and shifting as they grew into their proper places.

I hit the side of the cabinet and began to toboggan down the front toward the floor. I hid under the seat. It reminded me of the hair salon where I witnessed a huge fight with a water dragon, but I shook off the memories. I had bigger battles to face.

The floor, wet and sticky from the tea, caused my new-formed feet to stick to it.

Rotsen, climbing down out of Ralb's helmet, slithered down the arm of the chair and across to where I sat.

My feet were the next to take shape, and when I glanced down at my newly formed toes, I was reminded I desperately needed a pedi. A quick glance at my fingers, now fully evolved, revealed I also needed to book a mani. Great! On top of everything else, the powers that be on my home planet hadn't had the foresight to have these appendages ready painted and buffed.

"Oas, over here!" Rotsen said as I headed toward Ralb's chair.

I scrambled across the floor, feeling like I was in a fun house in a turning barrel. I was altering in shape in a container zooming through space, flipping and flopping like a full load in a washing machine. I had to skirt the broken mug to avoid cutting my foot.

Luckily the three humans (well one wannabe) were

too self-centered to realize what was going on in their midst. I hid from the cameras. I didn't want Ikey getting a look at me in mid-formation. It would be enough to make him lose his lunch.

"Get your *hanaglug* open!" Rotsen ordered when I reached him on the sticky, tea-stained floor.

"I don't have it."

"Where the heck is it?" Rotsen fumed.

"It's in the cage with Kaj," I said. "I got out of there so fast, I forgot it, and I knew if I went back in, she'd kill me. She can't get the case open, so it's safe in there."

"Geez, do I have to do everything?" Without waiting for an answer, he slinked across the floor, slipping in the tea before squeezing through the crack in the door and heading downstairs.

I crouched as I waited for him and was more than relieved when he came back.

Too sore and tired to argue, I opened it for him and watched as poked through the contents.

"This is a pretty measly packing job for a space traveler," Rotsen said. "If it was me, I'd have two flashlights, three packs of matches, seven vials in case the water was undrinkable, and suntan oil in case we ventured too close to the red globe."

"Just chillax," I said as my torso began to take shape. "Rotsen, do something."

"At least you had the brains to pack bobby pins." Wow, who knew he could actually praise me for something. I didn't want to tell him they were for my bangs, badly in need of a haircut. I'd only brought them in case I needed to tuck my hair out of my Earth-mode eyes.

"Before you shift into complete humanoid shape, we're going to pick the lock on that cabinet, and you're going to suck in everything possible and fit into it." Rotsen used his petals to pick apart the bobby pin so it was now in a V-shape.

Warily, I eyed the cabinet. The door was roughly three–feet-by-five-feet. I wouldn't be able to fit in there even if I suddenly became a super skinny supermodel.

Rotsen strolled across the distance, his stem sticking to the floor, so the noise was like the clip-clopping of a miniature horse.

"Hurry up," I begged as I felt more alterations occurring. The first time this happened on my way to Earth I'd been excited about the changes, plus I'd been traveling at warp speed through black holes and ended up with Peddy Bundt hair. Don't ask! And don't remind me I requested the look and style. What can I say? I was hooked on *Living with My Children,* and I didn't have that great a relationship with my own mother, through no fault of hers. If you had over five hundred plus children, you'd find it hard to pay attention to them all too.

Suzzy's thumbs were still flying across her small keyboard like they were on fire. My caring and thoughtful brother laughed out loud as he leaned across his seat so he could read her blog.

"You are a silly goose, saying I'm a hot guy." He grinned as he punched her arm. Snap! What was he? In grade school? Nice of him to keep her distracted. Next, he'd be pulling her hair and friending her on the Internet.

Rotsen on the other petal was working like a master safe cracker, unlocking the door. I was afraid everyone on board would hear my sigh of relief when it sprung open.

I waddled across the floor, my hands and feet humanoid, but the rest of me was still mantis. I crammed myself into the cabinet, just getting my tush inside before Rotsen slammed the door shut on me. In the dark, I felt around with my newly formed hands to see who or what were my cabin partners, though nothing could be worse than sharing a cage with Kaj. I was squeezed in beside life jackets, an inflatable boat, which I had to be careful not to push too hard against to keep it from springing into shape, and a very uncomfortable cardboard object which I couldn't identify. The room was dark and smelly, but whatever the article was it was pressing into my back and giving me a major bruise.

The more I morphed into human shape, the less room I had in the closet. It had been cramped when I was only hands and feet, now my torso was expanding the space was decreasing, big time. I felt like a pretzel. Like one of those girls in the magician's act who gets cut in half and has to squeeze into the bottom of the box to avoid the saws. Oh come on, you knew there had to be a trick to it, didn't you? I mean a magician would go through an awful lot of assistants if each time the act was on they got cut up. Plus, not too many people would apply for the job to begin with. I have to tell you though, Ralb thought it was real. Enough said there.

My torso filled out along with my head. In a mere matter of half an hour, I had returned to human form. I grasped my hair, pleased to see it was shoulder length and that my feet were covered in deck shoes. Great! Perfect in case I had to run somewhere. My legs, I used to call them walking sticks, were covered in denim, and I hoped I wasn't wearing overalls—not that I have anything against them, but they really aren't high fashion. Not that I was trying to impress anyone, but you should always look your best, FYI.

I was complete.

My newly developed foot fell asleep, but when I straightened out my cramped toes, I inadvertently pushed against the door, causing it to snap open loudly and ricochet against the metal wall. The sound echoed through the room, and the door banged open and shut again, hitting the side of the capsule like a home run ball smacking off an aluminum bat.

Not good.

Not good at all.

I cringed as all eyes turned in my direction and I prepared for the worse.

Luckily, I seemed to be shadowed by the darkness of my cave because the words from Suzzy were not the ones I had expected.

"Beau, look over there. What the heck is a weed doing on our ship?" Suzzy screamed. "You know I have a weed phobia, get it out of here right now."

"Now, Suzzy, you know what your therapist told you," Beau said. "You know I'm not supposed to enable you. Anything you want done, you have to do yourself so you will feel empowered."

"Wait!" Ralb cried out.

With a quickness Jack Chant would be proud of, Suzzy reached over, grabbed Rotsen's stem and scrunched him up, pulling each and every one of his petals off. She clapped her hands together, with Rotsen in the middle.

Ralb looked on, his visor up, his face mirroring what I felt. Once again, he stood by as Suzzy killed one of our friends.

First, she killed my mawlfriend, and now my only friend on this stupid spaceship.

She has totally messed with the wrong alien-slash-mantis-slash-person.

This means *war*!

Chapter 30

Ralb popped out of his chair. His suit was so massive and puffy he looked like a sumo wrestler. Okay, now my bro was going to sprint into action. Now everyone on this spaceship would be in awe of alien power. Sometimes Ralb's words could be a little cutting, sometimes his comments were a tad sharp and callous, but for the most part, he was kind, in a demented kind of way. But now we'd rule the cosmos once again. He would avenge the death of Josh and the recent murder of Rotsen, a poor helpless flower who never hurt anyone or anything.

I waited and held my breath, not an easy thing to do since I was crammed into the closet and a little out of breath to begin with. Okay, once I picked one species or the other for a while, I would hit the gym, and not just to sit on the machines and pretend like I was working out, unlike some siblings I could name.

Gently he picked up Rotsen from where Suzzy had tossed him onto the floor, and with gentleness I didn't know he'd possessed, tucked him into the breast pocket on his spacesuit. Ralb flipped down the visor of his helmet, and when he saw I was still safe and sound inside the cabinet pushed the door shut. The clasp didn't quite catch, though, so the door swung open as we took a tumble.

"Sorry, Suzzy," Ralb said as the spaceship shifted

to the left. He smashed his white gloved hand through the console, punching through a row of buttons as lights flashed and a puff of smoke erupted. He wiped his left hand on his thigh, and leaving a tea-colored stain advanced to the other console and started pushing random buttons.

"Dude, what do you think you're doing?" Beau asked. "Are you trying to kill us?" He gripped the arm rests. If I'd been in a happier mood, I might have gone to comfort him, but he looked like he had enough problems without wondering where the heck I came from. Besides, with what I'd just gone through, I wasn't in the mood to explain.

"Hey, man," Ikey's voice yelled from the monitor. "What do you think you're doing? Our mission is to just fly up and back down. You've short circuited the control panel."

Suzzy screamed. "I'm not meant for high altitude flying. I wasn't certified to go higher than an airplane." She paused, her hands at her throat. "I can't breathe. I'm breathless. Help! What is this going to do to my hair? I have to be back on Earth tonight, I have scripts to read and a television interview at seven o'clock."

Wow, glad to see her ducks were in a row, priority-wise.

You have to be trained for space travel. Maybe she just wasn't cut out for the reality show biz. She was the type of star who wanted Rodeo Drive and caviar, not the Milky Way. Heck, she'd probably say it was too fattening and would make her face break out big time. Let's face it, space travel isn't like booking a first-class flight on a commercial airline where they serve gourmet food and give you warm, moist towels to clean up with.

The spaceship tilted left.

Then right, then left, then upside down. The spilled tea gurgled and slopped around the floor, creeping into the edges where the walls met the floor.

Then left again. I felt like I was on a rollercoaster ride without a seatbelt.

Up we went, then plummeted right back down like an anchor tossed overboard. Faster we spiraled downward. My head smacked against the side of the cabinet, and the object which had annoyed me so recently now lodged permanently in my left side. I pressed my hands against the walls of the cabinet, trying to brace myself as the rocket fell.

Faster and faster we nosedived.

The door swung open again. I saw Ralb plastered against Suzzy, both of them wedged into her seat face-to-face or rather helmet-to-helmet, before the door shut again.

Beau was pressed into his own seat, his knuckles white and his clenched hands wrapped around the armrests like he was about to undergo dental surgery without any painkillers.

Something niggled at the back of my human brain, and it wasn't good. What was it? Something I had to do, something I needed to do?

Endlessly we continued downward. Really, who knew we were up so high? I guess it was like spilling a glass of water on the floor. You never knew how much was in it until you had to clean it up. I remember once on Zorca-twenty-three my Parental Being made a mess cooking, and there was sauce all over the floor from a spilled can.

It had reminded me of blood—not a pretty sight.

Kind of like an operation gone wrong….

Oh *snap*!

I kicked open the door of my secret cave and tried to stand up. I threw caution, and everything else, to the wind to try to get their attention. Everyone ignored me, so wrapped up in their own dilemma they didn't care about me. Rightly so I guess as to up until now they didn't know I existed in this metal utopia.

Stomping my feet and slamming my hand into the console, I tried to convey my message. My voice came out in a squeak.

"Ralb, what were you thinking? Why are you trying to sabotage us?" I yelled. "I thought you were trying to get us home!"

I was used to the sudden shifts in atmosphere, not to mention the seesawing of our ride, but I wasn't conditioned to standing up while we were tilting.

I flew into Beau's lap. His hands circled my slim waist as he caught me against his warm padded suit.

Trying to breathe, I pried his tight clasp loose, only to have him pull me close again. I really didn't mind, and at any other time I would have relished (and ketchuped) his embrace, but for once I had more important issues on my mind. A mind I wouldn't have much longer if I didn't do something immediately.

I grasped his visor, flipped it open, and gazed into his eyes.

"Beau, I need to find a helmet, or my head will explode."

Chapter 31

Without a thought to his own safety, he let go of me and unsnapped his chinstrap and plunked his helmet onto my head. Then his arms snaked around me, falling into their now familiar spots.

I struggled to take it off, to put it back on his head, but he kept my hands pressed to my sides. I inhaled in frustration, and the warm scent of his aftershave filled my nostrils. The smell represented safety and comfort, the same scent Josh wore.

"No, I insist. Least I can do since you snuck on here to see me. I'm so flattered." he said, apparently unaware the effect his scent was having on my senses. Man, talk about an alluring aroma. Whoever developed that fragrance sure knew what they were doing when they mixed all those scents. I was getting hot, and I don't think it had anything to do with the temperature in the room.

Wow, and here I thought chivalry was dead. But it was alive and well in this soon to be dead man. And he didn't seem at all inquisitive as to where I'd popped out from.

"Oas, eh, April." Ralb broke away from Suzzy and pointed at my head. "Give Beau back his helmet."

We hit a bump and then rocketed sideways, pressing us back in our seats.

"He won't let me," I said through clenched teeth.

"What can we do? I can't be responsible for his head exploding."

"I'll be right back." Ralb weaved toward the cupboard I had been hiding in. He had to walk sideways like he was in one of those old movies where people walked on the wall. Coming in from the top, he leaned down and pulled the door open, yanking the contents out, which fell onto the ceiling due to upside downiness.

The life raft jammed against the roof, and I held my breath that it wouldn't puncture. We might need it. The rate we were flying through clouds and space, we might crash land in the water. Having been a veteran of water landings and being on the receiving end of a rooney at Mach five, it's not a pleasant feeling. You experience the worst case of numb bum you can imagine. Major bum rush!

Wiggling out of Beau's grasp, I took the helmet and, before he could utter a word, plopped it onto his head and re-snapped the chin strap.

"Please, keep it on," I said as I watched Ralb and prepared for the worse.

"Found it." Ralb crab-crawled over to us, two silver disks in his hands. "Here! Clamp them on either side of your ears. You can't afford to have your ears pop or your brain will sizzle out the orifices."

Reluctantly I did as I was told. With a roll of duct tape, he wrapped the two mini satellite dishes to me, winding tape down around my chin and back up through my hair. Around and around he went, until I was like a twenty-third century mummy. I caught a glimpse of myself in a mirrored surface and shrieked.

Barely able to open my mouth, I forced my jaw to

form words. "Ralb, I'm going to kill you!! I look like someone from an alien movie, and not in a good way." I was a total satellite sandwich, and I had my dear darling brother to thank for that.

"Hey, I think you look cute." Beau grinned through his visor. "Everyone else pales in comparison to you." His arms tightened around my waist. "I'll make sure you get through this safe and sound, so hang on to me, babe."

Ralb snorted and continued to crab-walk along the ceiling until he was able to flop back into his seat and fasten his seat belt.

The screens in front of us sizzled and cracked. The picture of Ikey was replaced by the test screen and an annoying buzzing noise, reminiscent of the vuvuzela horn of South Africa.

I couldn't tell which way we were traveling—if we were upright or upside down. Now I know how pilots get disoriented. I peeked around Beau's head to check outside the window, but all I saw were clouds, some of them black and ominous, not a good sign for any type of traveling.

"Ralb, would you make this stop?" Suzzy said, her knuckles white.

I waited for my brother to tell her it wasn't like an amusement park ride where you could just hit the button and it all would be over but the barfing, but the wiener he is, he just patted her hand.

Big time wiener!

Yep, little Miss Suzzy had had enough, and it became evident when she leaned over her chair and tossed her cookies as well as her champagne and, from what I could determine, chunks of pineapple vomit. Of course, when she inclined over, she was out of camera range.

Not a pretty sight, not to mention smell. If I only had thought to bring my camera, I could have made a pretty penny selling a picture to the highest tabloid bidder.

Hey, I know it's petty and immature of me but, in my defense, remember she'd killed my mawlfriend and tortured my dandelion. All bets were off.

She looked greener than an ogre, and I couldn't believe her tiny stomach could hold so much liquid. Up she spewed again, and the vomit smell permeated our small, enclosed space. I don't know about you, but the odor of someone else's sickness is enough to make me want to hurl, but I concentrated on Beau's eyes, and my stomach settled.

"You feeling okay, babe?" Beau asked as he stroked my arm and then moved his hand up to my metal cymbals and pinged one with his index finger. He laughed, and I grinned as the sound vibrated.

"Stop that!" I laughed, trying to catch my breath at the absurdity of the situation. Here I was a teenage alien and this cute Earthling had me seesawing between hating him and wanting to—well you can imagine. It must be due to the humanoid hormones raging through my system. Throw in my annoying brother, a country-twanging teen star, and a spaceship, and basically you have my life up to this point.

I love Josh, I love Josh. I'm only doing this to revive Josh. I repeated the words to myself. Why on earth then did I have feelings for Beau? What is wrong with me? All these feelings were so alien, I was behaving like a mawl. I was behaving like Ralb.

"You can't make me." Beau smiled as he flipped his finger against my disks again. Why did he keep doing it?

"Beau, I'm warning you," I said feebly.

"Or you'll do what?"

"I'll—"

"Hey, do you guys hear that?" Ralb asked, as he tried to stand up, instead staggering like a drunk.

"Ralb, you idiot, I don't hear anything." I was sick of his stupid games. I wanted to get out of this contraption, out of this stupid headgear that was worse than archaic metal braces, and into a nice hot bath with a lot of bubbles.

"We're not spinning out of control, not hitting any more bumps." When he knew he had our attention, Ralb continued, "We're not listening to the wheezing or buzzing from the out-of-control television screen." Ralb clearly enjoyed being the center of attention. "Guys and gals, I think we've landed."

"But I didn't feel a splash. I didn't feel a thump of any kind," I whispered in awe. How could a metal spaceship that weighed ten times as much as a car land without so much as a blip?

"Don't you know anything?" Suzzy asked. "Parachutes release when we fall to a certain level to provide drag so we land smoothly."

"Well, excuse me for not being up on TZZ 101." I wanted to tell her my planet of Zorca-twenty-three is so far ahead of hers we didn't need drag to slow down our spaceships. We only had to set our minds to what we wanted it to do and presto, we landed. That's if we didn't catch a ride on a passing asteroid, which I can tell you is a major ride.

"Right, sorry, I must have missed the memo." I smiled over at her, only because I happen to notice the front of her jumpsuit was covered in yellow-and-green vomit.

Seemingly surprised by my kindness, she smiled back. Hey, maybe we could be friends after all. I just had to get over the fact she was a serial murderer.

I reached the next level of the spaceship and squawking noises filled the air. I tucked my hair behind my ears and wiped a bead of sweat with my right hand while the other hung onto the railing for balance. I slowly walked down the rest of the stairs.

I stopped on the last stair and sat down in disbelief onto the metal.

In front of me was bedlam.

Absolute mayhem!

The temperature had risen, and the Rockhopper penguins were leap frogging over each other in no apparent order. The monkey clapped its hands in glee as the butterflies dive bombed each of the cages.

"Where did you go?" Beau asked behind me. "I know you can't go far on the ship, but I wondered where you'd got to, babe. What the heck is going on down here?"

"Looks like the room warmed up and the Rockhopper's are well, hopping." A fit of giggles overtook me as Beau joined in.

Dodging penguins and butterflies, I walked over towards the cage that had held Kaj. The door hung open and there was no sign of the scaly lizard. I rustled through the shavings for the tissue containing Josh but it wasn't there.

There was no sign of Josh…or Kaj. I wasn't scared

of her now that I was at least seven times her size, but I admit the jaws of a Chuckwalla lizard were not to be tampered with.

It was empty. The lizard was gone and the tissue I'd left Josh tucked up in was shredded, like confetti.

Josh had been murdered. Again.

And it was all my fault. While I had been canoodling with Beau, Josh had been dinner. Karma is sure biting me in the butt, big time.

Chapter 32

"Hey, why the tears?" Beau turned me toward him and wiped away my waterworks with his thumbs. "I'm sorry, I always seem to do or say the wrong thing where you're concerned." He rested his arms on my shoulders. "You make me so nervous I—"

"No, it's not you," I interrupted him. "It's Josh. I knew he was dead, but I can't forget it was entirely my fault."

Ralb and Suzzy came into the room, stopped talking, and stared at us.

I knew my life had to go on, and I did kind of like Beau. I mean, what's not to like—he was kind, thoughtful, and could put Suzzy in her place. Plus, he smelt like Josh. Nothing I did or said would bring Josh back. I was never getting back to Zorca-twenty-three. There was no chance to revive Josh. I had to face facts. I had to go on with my own life. I had to pick up the pieces of my broken heart and proceed.

The first thing I had to do was get these stupid metal dinner plates off my head. I couldn't look sexy and cute for Beau with this stupid contraption covering my ears. I picked at the end of the tape and began to unravel it. Pain tore through my scalp when I got to the bottom where the adhesive was attached to my hair. The tape pulled my hair out by the roots, and once again my eyes welled up.

"You know what," Beau said, misinterpreting my renewed sadness. "I can't compete with a dead man. When you're ready for me to come into your life, let me know, and I might be around. But I've got to tell you, I'm not going to wait forever."

"Beau, wait! There's no need. Please give me a chance," I said.

My mind swirled as much as my stomach had done for the past couple of hours. I loved Josh with all my heart but I couldn't save him.

I'd failed.

Big time.

I didn't get him back to Zorca-twenty-three in time for Zen to work his magic. He was gone.

Josh, please forgive me.

Sobs racked through my body, and I dropped to my knees, sobbing. Strong arms lifted me up and then encased me. Beau lifted my head with his finger and searched into my soul with his eyes.

Then, I did something I'd never done before. With rejection staring me in my face, I reached up, removed Beau's helmet, and kissed him.

Right in front of Ralb. Right in front of Suzzy.

It was the kiss to signal new beginnings. It was a kiss like none other I'd ever shared. It was a promise.

His lips were tender and soft, and his tongue darted inside my mouth, not gross like, not all wet and slimy like a snake, but just nice. Whatever he was doing affected my stomach—not because of the wild spaceship ride, but it was flip-flopping in rhythm with his tongue.

I moaned as he loosened his grip and we continued to stand as one. With Beau's arms resting on my hips, I investigated the cage again. Where the heck could they have disappeared to? Well, actually I kind of figured I knew where Josh was—inside Kaj's digestive system—but where could that smelly lizard be?

"Come on," Ralb said. "Let's go and find out where we are."

From what I could see out the window, a bleak landscape awaited us. I had no idea where we'd landed, but it wasn't Zorca-twenty-three, or what I've seen of Earth, for that matter. One of the monitors began to hum and buzz annoyingly.

Lights flashed and bleeped continuously as I replayed Beau's kiss. I wanted to kiss him again, but I knew we had to get ourselves out of this mess.

It sure didn't seem like we were on Zorca-twenty-three. For one thing, our weather is a heck of a lot better. We don't have snow or any temps below seventy degrees Fahrenheit. We like to call ourselves the Florida of the solar system, but without the old people.

A cold breeze ruffled in through the cracks in the shell of our spaceship. It was frigid, which reminded me we weren't prepared for winter weather. I for one didn't bring cold weather clothes, but heck we had a life raft we could use to slide down any snow-covered mountains. I inched closer to Beau, making use of his body heat, wanting to get even closer. I mean, would you rather put on a winter coat or suck up the body heat of a hunk? Maybe we could find a nice warm fire somewhere and a bearskin rug. Just a thought.

"Can we get out of here and investigate the area?" Ralb asked. "We're off the radar, and we need to get help." He pointed to the blank television screens still spewing white noise.

Sure, now he was turning into Mr. Adventure, and Suzzy was acting like she was super keen. She looked like a cat that'd swallowed the cream in one lap without even choking.

Suzzy laughed. "Right, yes, let's get outside and see where we are," she said in a sing song voice. "Let's go out and see, see, see."

Alrighty, then.

"Hey, don't forget us." The voice behind me was the one I'd heard in my nightmarish time in the cage. I turned. Kaj had morphed into a super tall humanoid with braids down her back I would kill for.

"Kaj?" Ralb said, his chin dropping to his chest, his mouth gaping open. "How did you get here?"

"Geez, don't you listen? Hello! She was in the cage with me."

"You were in the cage?" Beau asked.

"I volunteered to come, to bring you two home."

Yeah, right, and I have land in Florida for sale. What's this line of bologna she's spewing?

Now I was the one with the open mouth. Liar, liar, pants on fire. She was such a liar head.

"No, really why did you come?" Ralb continued. "Zen wouldn't send you to bring us home."

"Okay, I wanted to see for myself what all the fuss was about your sister."

"She's beautiful," said the mawl standing beside her.

His brown eyes were the color of tree trunks, and he wore a baseball cap backward over his brown, curly hair.

"Hi, April, nice to see you again," Josh whispered to me as his glance took in Beau, whose arm was still encircling my waist. "I guess I don't have to ask you what you've been up to since I last saw you." Like the gentleman he was, he stretched out his hand to Beau. "I'm Josh."

"Hey, man, I thought you were dead?" Beau looked from Josh to me, then back to Josh again. "Where did you come from man?

"It's a long story, for another time." I inched further away from Beau.

I couldn't help myself. I ran to Josh and jumped into his arms, wrapping my newly formed legs around his torso. "I can't believe you're okay."

He put me back on the ground like I was toxic. Hurt raced across his face, and his eyes were wounded as if he'd lost the love of his life.

My heart ached with nostalgia, and the hot wave that swept through my body at his touch turned into iciness.

Ralb held up his hands, glancing between Josh and an angry Beau. "Hey, guys, she's my sister, and she's definitely not worth getting into a fight over."

"I don't have any intention of fighting for her," Beau replied calmly. "It's obvious she's made her decision, and it wasn't me."

"But how did you switch? What happened? Last I saw you were in the cage with Kaj and well, deader than a doorknob."

"When you put me in the *hanaglug*, some of the pills rolled around in the case and rubbed up against my skin. Well, they must be pretty strong chemicals, 'cause here I am. None the worse for wear and tear." Josh turned and took a little bow.

We didn't need *Remmo*.

I remembered now Xron had given me a pile of pills and had muttered something about pills for mawls and how he was out of them for femawls, which I figured was par for the course. Looking back, I now wondered why with zero-gravity they didn't float up to the ceiling but instead stayed on the floor. I'd have to ask Xron when I got back, but first things second.

Now getting back to Josh, how cool he knew Zorcan-twenty-three terms, but I couldn't look at him. I felt rather than saw the tears welling in his eyes.

Suzzy broke the tension. "Come on, Josh, let's go and investigate our new surroundings." She took his arm in hers and winked at us over his shoulder. "You know, Josh, I always did have a crush on you in Bedrocktown."

With that comment hanging in the air, she dramatically yanked open the door of the spaceship. A blast of snow rained down on us, drifting through the door.

"I'm shutting the frigging door." Ralb called out, a hangdog expression on his face, dejected from going from first to worst in the race for Suzzy's heart.

I ran up the stairs to the cabinet which had been my hidey hole for the flight and rooted around inside, trying to find something warm. The best I could come up with were life jackets, so I quickly put one on and handed one to Kaj. The others at least had their spacesuits to keep themselves toasty, but we only had the clothes on our back, front, and legs. I should have listened to my Parental Being, she told me to pack a coat 'cause she said it might get cold. Great, now I'll never hear the end of it.

"What?" I asked as Kaj and Beau frowned at me. "I

have to do something to keep warm and no"—I held up my hand to Beau— "I know what you have in mind, but right now we have to concentrate on figuring out where we are and how to get back to where we should be."

"Good point, though it is frigging cold out there," Ralb said. "Kaj, can you help me get the door?" He pulled it open against the wind, and with her help slid it along the track so it remained unfastened.

A burst of fresh, freezing air whipped inside the capsule, and it took a minute for me to catch my breath. Everyone's breath hung in the air like a frosty fog.

I poked my head outside and immediately covered my ears with my hands as my nose turned red and my cheeks rosy. "I don't see Suzzy or Josh anywhere." I glanced down. "There aren't even any tracks outside the spaceship." I shivered. The life jacket provided no warmth. It didn't even cut the wind. "Where could they have gone?"

Beau and Kaj stepped toward the door, but I held up a finger. "Shh. I think I hear something."

"I hope it's not the Abominable Snowman coming to eat us," Kaj said, smirking, obviously not caring I'd just asked her to be quiet. Besides, who's she to talk about eating us when she'd been flapping her jaws when I was in the cage with her? Now everything changed since she was on the other end of the food chain.

"Yeah, right. Geez, what books have you been reading? Everyone knows the Abominable Snowman is not real." I felt like smacking her across the back of the head. What a great image to put into someone's mind— mainly mine.

My teeth chattered, and my nose started to drip. I

was comforted by Beau's arms as they enveloped me, but a constant tapping on the side of the ship began to unnerve me.

Rat-a-tap-tap. Tap! Tap! Tap!

"What the heck is that noise?" Kaj asked. "It's really getting on my nerves, and I haven't had caffeine for the past week. If I don't get some soon, I'm not going to be held responsible for my actions." Her head flung around left to right, and I took a step backward to get out of her line of sight.

Again, the tapping continued.

"Ralb, why don't you man up and go and see what the heck that noise is?" Kaj taunted my brother.

"If you're so brave, why don't you?" he yelled back at her. "You're man enough for both of us."

Oh no!

"Stop." Beau defused the situation by holding up his hand like a traffic cop. "Never mind, you two. I don't want to clean up the blood. I'll go and investigate what the noise is." Without another word, Beau headed toward the open door and peered out. He jumped down into the snow, and the next I heard instead of the tapping noises was a man yelling.

Curiosity overtook my fear, and I inched my way toward the opening. Snow continued to swirl inside the container, and I bent down to pick up a handful. I licked the snow cautiously. In my heart I was still an alien and wanted to try new things. I just wouldn't be putting my tongue on a shovel anytime soon, though I might encourage Ralb to. Last time I ate something so cold, I was the recipient of a major brain freeze.

"April, you've got to come and see this," Ralb called, his voice sounding slightly muffled.

I leaned out the door, lost my balance, and fell face first into a soft but cold snowdrift. I pushed myself up on my hands. My clothes were soaked, and I could easily win first place in a wet T-shirt contest, even though my breasts and nipples were frozen solid. Water lay in front of me, the edges frozen solid.

Eyes met mine, and I screamed. I scrambled backward, and my body hit a black-and-white mini fire hydrant.

"Aren't they the cutest?" Beau asked as he stroked the closest animal. "I just love penguins."

Black-and-white tuxedoed birds swam like mini torpedoes, diving off my snowbank before waddling out of the water and sliding down the mound back into the water. Even cold and wet, I couldn't stop myself laughing at their antics.

A particularly large bird that looked to be around seventy-five pounds seemed to believe I was either its mother or, yikes, maybe its mate, and snuggled under my arm, apparently seeking what little body heat I emanated. I read somewhere penguins mate for life, but I wasn't about to spend eternity in this environment.

"Looks like you've found a friend." Beau laughed. "My guess is he wants you for a girlfriend. You can be the queen of the rookery." He bent over, tears of laughter freezing on his face.

One curious penguin hopped onto the spaceship and began barking at the animated one, its barking gradually increasing in volume as it continued to receive no response.

"Typical female, totally ignoring the male," Beau joked. "Did you know that they have twelve feathers per square centimeter?"

"Very funny." I tried to stand, and Beau reached a hand down to help me up. My bird friend took a swipe at his hand, nearly breaking the skin. "I'm going to call him Derex." Seemingly, he knew his name as my penguin turned and glanced at me with moony eyes.

Nudging me along, the penguin forced me to walk away from Beau and away from the spaceship. We climbed a mound of snow to where Josh and Suzzy were standing, her arm wrapped around him like he was the finest birthday present. Beau joined us as well, and we stood looking down the bank at a disaster.

The smell was what overwhelmed me first. The stinky, yucky smell of oil. Oil lapping up against the once pure snow. Corpses of baby penguins, as well as krill and jellyfish, bobbed and flowed as the tide moved in and out.

"I heard about this on the news," Beau said. "It's a major oil spill off the coast of New Zealand. Environmentalists are concerned about the effect it's going to have on future generations of wildlife."

Suzzy began to cry. "I've never seen anything so horrible. What are we going to do?"

Three heads turned and faced me.

"What?"

"You're always listening to your *wad*, watching those time-wasting educational programs," Ralb said.

"And you did save Nicola's life when she got sick with *E. coli*," Suzzy admitted grudgingly.

"But that was easy." Even as I spoke, I knew I had to do something. I couldn't stand by and watch this mess. I had to try something.

"Wait here," I said as I hopped back into the spaceship. "Rotsen, you have to help me," I called out to his spirit. "We have a major problem here, and I need you." I closed my eyes and pictured Rotsen until he was right in front of me, totally life-like.

"Use the *mist book*."

Right. I pulled open my *hanaglug* and dug out my *mist book*, ignoring the pills and other items.

Flipping through the pages, I bypassed the dandelions page. I'd get back to that, but first things first.

Wow, this book was a bible, so to speak, on earth matters. There weren't any subjects it didn't explain. I gathered together what I needed and with energy ran from the room.

When I traveled via asteroid to your planet, I had the company of the annoying unicells. Well, it turns out on earth, they're called microbes and they like to eat oil. Who knew?

"Okay, folks." I jumped down from the spaceship and ran toward the group, sliding down the slope. "Here's what we need to do."

The group gathered around me as I explained my plan, even the penguins listened up. It seemed too easy, but then the best plans often were.

"Ralb is going to collect as many uni-microbes as possible with the help of our penguin friends who know where they hang out. Then we're going to take them out into the ocean and let them loose to eat the oil to their hearts' content and their stomachs are full. Next, we're going to use Suzzy's gum to soak up the residue on the penguins and other animals in the area and, fingers crossed, the problem should be under control."

"So, you're saying my gum is going to save the day?" Suzzy asked.

"I know, I find it hard to believe, but black currants contain a high concentration of Omega-3, and that's something oil hates. Did you ever try the experiment where you mix oil and water to see how they separate?" Heads nodded, even Derex's, so I continued, "Well, when you add black currants into the mix, it clots and forms blobs, easy to pick up."

"So how do we get the microbes out into the water?" Kaj asked, standing joined at the hip to Josh, who I was relieved to see inch away from her.

"Easily." I could tell my enthusiasm was contagious. "I'm going to float out in the raft and spread them over the thickest part of the oil. The areas I can't get to fast enough, the penguins swim under the oil and float the microbes upward." They nodded in unison. "Josh, Beau, head inside. By the cages are thirty cartons of gum. Bring them out. Also, we'll use the animated penguins to draw out the real ones."

Putting their jealousy on hold, companionably they walked into the spaceship and hauled out the boxes.

"What do you want us to do?" Suzzy asked.

"Get chewing." And with that I handed them each a wad of gum, and our lips began to smack.

Derex nudged my leg and when I looked down at him, he flapped his wings at me.

"No, I'm not giving you gum to chew. You don't know how to process it, and I don't want you to choke."

"Not going to happen, Oas!" Derex telepathed back to me.

I gave a startled gasp. "How did you do that?"

"You're not the first space traveler from Zorca-twenty-three." Derex smiled. "Though let me tell you, Antarctica wasn't my first choice."

I patted him on the head. "Then get chewing, my friend."

Epilogue

"So, tell us, Suzzy, how did you come up with such a unique idea on how to stop the oil flow?" a reporter asked, thrusting a microphone into her face.

I was exhausted. The events of the previous three nights had taken their toll on me. If I never see another piece of bubble gum it will be too soon. Happy to stay in the background, I leaned into Beau's shoulder and grinned when he kissed the top of my head.

"You should be up there, it was your idea," he whispered, nuzzling my ear, and sending goose bumps across my body and through my nether regions.

"Nah, she loves the spotlight." I smiled. "She can take the credit."

"Actually, it was my friend April who came up with the idea." Suzzy reached through the crowd and pulled me by the arm. "While I cried, she jumped into action and saved the penguins."

What? Suzzy was being nice. She didn't need to share the limelight. I wasn't interested in it, but she was giving me credit.

"She was the genius. She found a life raft and boxes of my gum, and she inflated it while we were busy chewing gum. She even called upon the penguins and got them to help." She paused. "My gum absorbed the oil out of the penguins and some bug, or something, cleaned up the oil spill." She paused again, either to catch her breath or for drama. Hey, she was my friend now, so I gave her the benefit of the doubt.

"What are your future plans?" another reporter asked.

"Well," Suzzy said, "we haven't really talked about it, but I'd like to work with April on other projects. We have meetings set up, but we can't speak of them until we have something concrete."

"Sounds like you're going to be busy." Beau wove his fingers through my hair. "Will you have time for me?"

"Yes, I think I might be able to fit you in, if for no other reason than to beat you in Space Monsters."

"No way! You're AprilOAS23?"

"You bet, mister, and you are so going down." I breathed deeply. Beau so didn't know the real me, the ALIEN me, and he wasn't going to. A girl has to keep some secrets.

Rotsen wobbled on his feet, still a little woozy from his life-after-death experience. "Kids, can't you think of something else to do besides play stupid video games?" His telepathing skills were weak, and he sounded like radio static.

"Hey, you." I patted his petal. "You owe me big time. Because of me and the *mist book* you have another life."

My *mist book* was worth its weight in meteorites. After we'd saved the penguins, I flipped through it and found the section that recommended rubbing the roots of any deceased plant with pumice. Taken from the Bay of Plenty, it only took a couple of rubbings before Rotsen began to stir and was soon back on his stem, back to his regular sarcastic self.

"I hate to remind you, but I'm the one who packed the book, and I'm the one who looked in it to save Nicola from *E. coli* poisoning in Bedrocktown." He paused, his breathing labored.

"Well, I'm glad I revived you. I can't take all the credit for saving Nicola." I flicked at his petals. Turning back to Beau, I linked my hand into his. "I want to place a bet on our Space Monsters game."

"Anything, babe."

"If I win, you quit smoking, once and for all." I reached up and kissed him on the cheek.

"And if I win, you marry me, or we at least live together."

Yikes, hold the mobile and any other contraption you might own. I have no intention, and I mean no intention, of getting married anytime soon. I had too much living to do. I had charities to help, places to see, and adventures to adventure. Not that I couldn't do that if I was married, but heck, it certainly wouldn't be as much fun.

Which told me one thing.

Or maybe two.

Definitely three.

Beau was not the mawl for me, but he did need to quit smoking. I glanced over toward Josh and caught his eye. His smile lit up his face, and I grinned back. Now there was a mawl who got me, and knew me, and loved me, alien secrets and all. "Beau, we need to talk," I said, watching Josh.

"I'm not letting you go without a fight."

Wow, two mawls fighting over this little teenage ALIEN. Does life get any better?

Little did I know it did and the adventures would continue....

A word about the author...

Born with a passion to read and write and heavily influenced by Nancy Drew mysteries, Jane Greenhill recalls her first writing experience on an old Underwood typewriter, plunking away at the keys while she wrote about hiding clues in oak trees. Fast forward through marriage and motherhood, and Jane's now advanced to a laptop and her characters speak to her from other planets.

Thank you for purchasing
this publication of The Wild Rose Press, Inc.

For questions or more information
contact us at
info@thewildrosepress.com.

The Wild Rose Press, Inc.
www.thewildrosepress.com

www.ingramcontent.com/pod-product-compliance
Lightning Source LLC
Chambersburg PA
CBHW061135200626
46817CB00016B/1535